THE WHISPERING KNIGHTS

Penelope Lively was born in Egypt in 1933. She read history at St Anne's College, Oxford, and is now married to an Oxford don. Mr and Mrs Lively have two school-age children, a son and a daughter, and live in a sixteenth-century farmhouse in Oxfordshire.

By the same author in Piccolo

ASTERCOTE

THE WHISPERING KNIGHTS

PENELOPE LIVELY

Cover illustration by Robin Lawrie
Text illustrations by Gareth Floyd

A PICCOLO BOOK

PAN BOOKS LTD : LONDON

First published 1971 by William Heinemann Ltd
This edition published 1973 by Pan Books Ltd,
33 Tothill Street, London SW1

ISBN 0 330 23671 7

Printed and Bound in England by
Hazell Watson & Viney Ltd,
Aylesbury, Bucks

To Mrs Winifred Williams of
Freeland Primary School

One

The frogs' legs were less appalling than the children had expected. They slid out of the tin with a plop, a slimy, grey-brown mass: very nasty, but not obviously legs. Martha was much relieved. She had expected pathetic little webbed feet at the ends.

'Seven and six for that lot!' said William with disgust. 'I jolly well hope they're worth it.'

Susie began stirring the saucepan. The frogs' legs quickly disintegrated and merely served as a kind of thickening. The pictures were coming to pieces too. The bird's wing floated suddenly to the surface and Martha averted her eyes.

'Are you sure it's all right?' she said uneasily. 'I wish we'd never done it.'

''Course it's all right, silly,' said Susie, her eyes on the pan. She stirred more vigorously and began to chant:

'Double, double toil and trouble,
Fire burn, and cauldron bubble.'

They had built the fire near the door of the barn, so that the smoke could go out, and also so that they could see what they were doing. The big double doors, built for farm wagons to drive through, were the only source of light, except for the cracks in the roof where slates were missing, and the row of ventilation holes high up in the end wall. The far corners were always murky and unexpected, with mounds of hay, mice, and bird droppings. It was only a very small fire, neat and tidy. William was fussy about fires: as he rightly said, there was no surer way of getting themselves forbidden to play in the barn than to set it on fire. Susie complained that it was too small.

'This thing's never going to boil,' she said crossly.

Martha sat back on her heels, twisting a strand of hair nervously round and round her fingers. She'd had doubts about this business, right from the start, but the others had insisted and, as usual, her fears had got brushed aside. It was a scientific experiment, William had said, not a spell. It's all very well saying that, Martha thought. You can call it what you like but it still sounds like a spell. And with these stories about the barn once being a witch's home, it all seemed most unsafe. Susie and William had always disregarded the witch stories, of course, but she'd been worried all the time when they first started playing in the barn, jumping when the wind rustled a heap of dead leaves on the worn stone floor, and staring at the dark folds of shadow in the corners.

'You don't really believe all that stuff, do you?' William used to say. 'Witches and that? There weren't ever such things, you know. It was just superstition. Trying to blame other people when things went wrong. Illnesses, and cows dying, and all that. My dad says, and he knows.' William's father was a schoolmaster.

'Well—' Martha remained unconvinced. 'Why do people in the village go on about it, then? Grown-ups. As though they half-believed it.'

'Huh!' said William, contemptuous. 'They get in a habit about saying some things, don't they? Just can't stop themselves. Or else they're trying to frighten you.'

Susie was unmoved, too. But then she was never

scared of anything. She wasn't that much older than Martha, but sometimes she seemed years older, so sure of herself, with her round face and the fat plait hanging down her back; plump and competent, like her mother who ran the village shop. Martha envied her. Susie was allowed to help in the shop, putting things in paper bags and then closing the bags with a quick twirl just like her mother, sorting out change and slapping it down on the counter, bustling about.

The saucepan gave a sudden heave and William peered into it with interest. 'Is it going to boil?' he asked, acknowledging Susie's superior knowledge of cooking.

Susie scowled at it doubtfully. 'It's still not hot enough. Put some more sticks on. Look, I can put a finger in it, it's that cold.' She stuck a finger in the grey mass, nearly licked it, and then thought better of it and wiped it on her frock instead.

The square of yellow sunlight falling on the barn floor from the open door faded quite suddenly, as though a light had been switched off. The flames, which had been visible only as a quivering in the air, turned orange and a thin trail of blue smoke drifted away and up into the shadowy places overhead where the great beams and rafters held up the stone slate roof. Martha, squatting on the cold stone floor, shivered.

'What do we do with it, anyway?' said Susie suddenly. 'What did the witches do with it when they'd made it?' She stared accusingly at William. It had been his idea in the first place.

William realized with embarrassment that he didn't know. The original idea had simply been to make a witch's brew in the place where a witch had once been (not, of course, that one believed all that stuff): the interest had lain in the difficulty of collecting together all the ingredients. Now that they had actually made the brew he couldn't remember at all what he had intended to do with it. I s'pose that happens to lots of scientists, he thought. They get carried away mixing stuff up together and then they can't remember what they did it for. Or else they make some great discovery quite by accident. He stared at the mixture, disappointed: it didn't look at all promising.

'Throw it away, I suppose,' he said lamely.

'Eat it, maybe,' said Susie, with a sideways glance at Martha, who choked violently. She remembered the first time William had come up to the barn with his idea, bursting with enthusiasm, a grubby scrap of paper clutched in his hand on which he'd written down all the things they'd need.

> 'Eye of newt, and toe of frog,
> Wool of bat, and tongue of dog,
> Adder's fork, and blind-worm's sting,
> Lizard's leg, and howlet's wing.'

'Are you daft?' Susie had said, with a flattening look. 'How can we get all those things? It's not like six ounces of flour and a quarter of butter and two ounces of sugar, is it? I don't call that a recipe at all. I don't think it would make up a bit well. Where did you get it?'

'It's in Shakespeare,' said William. 'My dad showed it to me. And we could get the things. Or near enough, anyway. We could use newt spawn for the eye of newt – after all it turns into whole newts in the end, so it's got eye of newt in it, hasn't it? There's tons in the pond back of Larkins' farm.'

'What about tongue of dog, then?' said Susie coldly. 'And adder's fork?'

Martha gazed from one to the other of them in horror. 'You can't,' she said. 'Not a real dog. You just can't.'

William frowned, and searched the horizon for inspiration. They had been sitting outside the barn at the time, leaning their backs against the sun-warmed stone, with the field sloping gently away in front of them towards the village. Behind them was the barn, with its rough stone walls that ran through every colour from soft grey to brilliant apricot, according to how the light struck them, and its old, sagging roof on which moss and lichen grew like green and gold fur. On the far side of the barn, almost hidden by trees and a high stone wall, was a big house, set apart from the village like the barn itself, isolated among the fields. Further away the grey roofs of the village houses lifted a little above the fields and the village noises drifted to them across the grass: a tractor grinding down the road, somebody hammering at the garage, the thumping engine of a lorry waiting outside the shop. And further away still, the fist-shapes of willows were strung out along the winding banks of the Sharnbrook.

'You know that old toy dog your baby brother's got, Susie?' said William carefully. 'It's got that great long pink felt tongue . . . Do you think he'd mind?'

Susie considered. Martha could feel her being gradually converted, even generating a tiny flame of enthusiasm. 'He don't hardly ever play with it,' she said. She and William stared steadily at each other. Conspiracy began to flower.

'And there's my snakeskin,' said William, 'for the adder's fork.'

'It would get spoilt,' said Martha desperately, with a final effort to control the rush of events. 'It's your most precious thing.'

'I don't care. And we could use a dead bird's wing for the howlet's wing. I daresay it doesn't matter if it isn't an owl really. There's often dead sparrows around.'

'The toe of a frog will be difficult,' said Susie with deliberation. 'A toy again?'

'We can do better than that,' said William triumphantly. 'You can get tins of frogs' legs. People eat them.'

The girls stared in disbelief. 'Don't be disgusting,' said Susie.

'Honestly. It's true. I saw an advertisement in dad's newspaper once. And tins of bees and chocolate-coated ants. Listen, could you get your mum to order some for the shop?'

Susie had doubts. 'I know what she'll say. She'll say there's no demand for them in Steeple Hampden.'

And she was right. Mrs Poulter was scornful. She could get rid of the odd packet or two of China tea, she said, and a few dozen frozen prawns now and then, and stem ginger at Christmas, but frogs' legs, no. In the end William had had to get the address from his father's newspaper and order them, at vast expense, from this shop in London. They'd all contributed out of their pocket-money.

The wool of a bat, the blind-worm's sting, and the lizard's leg had presented almost insuperable problems. They hunted unsuccessfully for dead lizards. William and Susie argued for hours about whether bats had wool or feathers, anyway. Susie favoured feathers and Martha, who knew she was wrong, sided with William and felt treacherous. She was usually with Susie over things, because of both being girls, and anyway William was cleverer than either of them. Not that that bothered Susie, who could win many an argument with sheer obstinacy.

In the end they had to draw careful pictures of a bat, the hindquarters of a lizard (from William's encyclopaedia) and a coiled slow-worm. It seemed unsatisfactory, but William said it would have to do and anyway making an image of something was a well-known way of magicking it.

Martha searched for reassurance. It couldn't work, surely, because they hadn't got all the things exactly right. Nothing would happen, really. 'What will happen?' she whispered.

'Nothing,' said Susie, stolidly. 'It's just for something to do.'

'I don't know,' said William. 'It's to find out.'

And now here they were, on a Tuesday morning in August, crouched over the saucepan while Susie stirred, with the soft bonfire smell drifting away out of the barn door, and with it another, less pleasant, smell. And the sun had gone right in so that the barn had got as dark as twilight, and a little wind had stirred and was sending twists of hay drifting over the stone flags and making strange sighing noises above their heads in the roof. The mess in the pan was getting hotter now, and steaming a little, and they were all staring fascinated at it, as though they expected something to get up out of it. Susie was scowling, as she so often did, and William was poking the pan with a stick and whistling through his teeth, and Martha was rocking backwards and forwards on her heels, frightened, with her thin, sharp shoulder-blades sticking up under her cotton dress like stumpy wings.

They were all so absorbed that they did not notice
that a fourth person had joined them. She was able
to stand in the doorway, watching them, for several
minutes, before any of them looked up.

At last she spoke. 'Haven't you forgotten something?
What about "Bubble, bubble, toil and trouble"?'

They all jumped. Martha, who was facing the door,

saw only the black shape of her, featureless because the light was all behind, and saw that she was old, and bent, and leaning on a stick. She gave a scream, half stifled because all the breath had gone out of her in a sudden panic. And then she buried her face in her hands, shivering.

William, sitting sideways, could see her face, and the light glinting on her glasses, and the silver knob of her stick, and the brooch that fastened her grey blouse at the throat. When his heart had stopped the wild thumping it had begun when she spoke, he did some quick sensible thinking and knew that it must be the old lady who lived in the house next to the barn. Miss Hepplewhite, wasn't she called? He peered at her face, trying to see her expression. This might mean trouble. This might mean no more playing in the barn.

Susie said flatly, 'I said it just now. I reckoned as how once would do.'

'I daresay,' said Miss Hepplewhite, stepping further into the barn.

Martha peeped through her fingers, and then began to take her hands away from her face. Miss Hepplewhite poked the empty tin of frogs' legs with the end of her stick and it rolled noisily on the stone floor. 'Ingenious,' she said. 'How did you manage the tongue of dog?'

They told her. She nodded once or twice, thoughtfully. You could not tell from her expression whether she approved or disapproved.

At last Martha said, in a shaky voice, 'Does it matter? Have we done anything wrong?'

The fire was beginning to die down into a pool of pale wood ash. The concoction in the saucepan had congealed into an unpleasant mass, and had certainly lost any appeal it ever had for them. Susie was eyeing it doubtfully and wondering if she was going to be able to scrape it out and get the saucepan cleaned up and back on the kitchen shelf before dinner. Outside, the wind had dropped and into a dark stillness came heavy drops of rain, like fingers tapping the leaves.

Miss Hepplewhite touched the ash with her stick. Feathery grey curls writhed, and fell apart. 'I don't know that you have done anything wrong,' she said. 'But you may have done something very unwise.'

They all looked at her, startled. Susie, beginning to collect things up, put the empty tin down again suddenly. Martha's stomach lurched again and she thought: 'I knew we shouldn't! I knew we shouldn't, but they wouldn't listen!'

William said, 'But it's all superstition. Witches and that. It was just for fun. There wasn't ever a witch here.'

'Really?' said Miss Hepplewhite. 'Then why all the talk? Down here . . .' She pointed with her stick in the direction of the village. 'A story that persists in that way must have some kind of substance, surely you'll agree?'

'But not a fairy-tale witch with a pointed hat and all that,' said William firmly. 'There never were any of those.'

'Quite,' said Miss Hepplewhite. 'I'm not disputing that.'

'Then what was there?' said Martha. She said it very quietly, almost to herself, because she was not at all sure that she wanted to hear the answer. 'Was there any-thing?'

Outside it was very dark now, and darker still in the

16

barn. The green of the field was bright against a grey sky, and the rain hissed quietly.

'Oh, there was something all right,' said Miss Hepplewhite, with what might have been a sigh. 'She was here, you see, for a time.'

'She?' said William. 'Who is she?'

Miss Hepplewhite looked at him curiously. 'Dear me, I would have expected you to know about her. I knew her pretty well at your age, but perhaps she is less familiar to children nowadays. She is Morgan le Fay, who was Arthur's sister and did all she could to destroy him, and Duessa, and Circe, and the Witch in Snow White, and the Ice Queen, and many, many others. She has had many disguises, and many tricks. She is from a time far older than ours, you see, but she is always here somewhere. Nowadays we hear less of her in her old forms. She may not have outgrown them, but we have, and she has had to think up other shapes. Sometimes I hardly know her myself, but in the end she always gives herself away. She is the bad side of things, you see.'

The children were quite still. Susie whispered, 'I say!' in a very low voice. Martha's eyes widened, but she was silent.

'How do you mean – she was here for a time?' asked William.

'It was one of her places. She had them – has them – everywhere. And then people gradually stopped believing in her and she had to go somewhere else. She feeds on credulity, you see. That is how she gets her foot in the door. But as soon as people begin to forget a little, and laugh when they say there was a witch in the old barn, instead of speaking with respect, then her time is up, and she must move on.'

'So she's quite gone now,' said Susie. She sounded relieved.

Miss Hepplewhite said nothing. She stood with her hands folded on the knob of her stick, staring at the ruin of the fire.

'Has she gone?' asked William, watching Miss Hepplewhite.

'I thought so,' said Miss Hepplewhite at last. 'There has been no sign of her for many, many years now. But she always has a feeling for places that have once been hers. She watches them. You may have reminded her of Steeple Hampden, and the valley.' She did not speak at all accusingly, merely as though certain things were inevitable.

In the corners of the barn, and in the shadowy places above their heads, there were rustlings and creakings. A little gust of wind sent a circle of leaves eddying across the flagstones, and dispersed the pale, soft ash of the fire. Martha said to herself firmly: 'It is nothing, the barn is always like this, it always moves and talks to itself.'

Miss Hepplewhite moved towards the door and the children followed her. It had stopped raining, but the sky was heavy, with steel grey, full-bellied clouds pressing down on the hills that ran along the sides of the valley, and slanting columns of rain reaching from sky to earth in the distance.

'Perhaps she put the sun out,' said William. It was not clear whether he meant it to be a joke or not.

'Oh no,' said Miss Hepplewhite. 'She never had much control over the weather. Though she's well able to turn it to her advantage.'

Somewhere a long way away thunder rolled across the sky.

Martha said, 'When we did it – the fire and everything, and the frogs' legs – we never really expected anything to happen. We didn't believe in her. So it won't matter, will it?'

'Didn't you?' said Miss Hepplewhite. 'None of you? Why do it, then?'

Martha looked at William, and her cheeks glowed, and William looked away. Susie stared firmly at the ground.

'Oh, well,' said Miss Hepplewhite. 'It was only a small belief, so I daresay no harm will come of it. In any case, she was always less interested in children. It is grown-ups she wants to get hold of.'

'How will we know?' asked Martha.

'Oh, you will know all right. She will be looking for your weaknesses, if she has noticed you at all. You will have to be on your guard. And now I must go.'

She turned and walked quickly away across the cobbled place beside the barn, towards the wall that surrounded her own garden, without saying goodbye or looking back towards them. Nevertheless she left the children with a strong feeling that she expected to see them again. There was a small green door in the wall, which she opened and walked through, closing it firmly behind her.

Martha watched her go, and suddenly became aware that she felt most uncomfortably cold. A numbing chill had spread through her whole body, so that her feet and legs felt quite detached, and her hands were stiff and bent, like little claws. She could not remember ever having felt quite like that before: it was almost a paralysis. It seemed in some unaccountable way to come from within; like feeling sad or happy. She looked over towards Susie, in alarm, and saw that Susie, plump

Susie, so well insulated by her own fat that she rarely wore a sweater even in winter, was convulsed with a fit of shivering.

As Martha looked at her, she put down the saucepan she was trying to clean out with some leaves and said in a cross voice, 'There's a goose walking over my grave.' She sounded exactly like her mother.

They both looked at William, who was staring at his own arm and rubbing it. 'Now I know how dogs feel when their hair stands on end,' he thought. 'Interesting.'

Aloud, he said, 'I'm frozen. Funny . . .'

'It's that old storm,' said Susie. 'A bit of rain can make it ever so cold all of a sudden. Let's go home.' She began to collect up their things.

William kicked the fire apart, to make sure it was properly out. 'That's it,' he said. 'It's the storm.'

'Oh,' said Martha, relieved. 'Are you sure?'

'Quite sure,' said William firmly. 'Come on.'

Once outside, warmth began to creep back into their limbs. A rainy sunshine was falling onto the roof of the barn so that faint wisps of steam rose from the slates.

Martha, hanging back a few paces behind the others, thought that with them rose a soft hissing noise, but then again it might have been the whisper of water running away along the gutter, or the leaves moving in the wind. She ran to catch the others up, and thought no more of it, as the blood ran back into her toes and fingers, and the sights and sounds of Steeple Hampden distracted her.

Two

Later that evening, sitting over tea at the kitchen table, Martha mentioned the meeting with Miss Hepplewhite. The rest, obviously, she kept to herself.

'She still up there?' said Martha's father in surprise. He had just come in from milking and sat steaming slightly in the warmth of the kitchen, his hair beaded with damp. The rain had been around all day. 'She must be getting on now. I remember her when I was a boy, and she weren't young then. You'd best keep on the right side of her, if you want to play up in that old barn. It's her property, you know.'

'Is it?' said Martha in surprise. 'She never said. We never thought about whose barn it was.'

The children were used to being chivvied from one place to another in the village: keep off my field, and don't play around my farmyard, and stop making that noise outside my house. She felt a new warmth towards Miss Hepplewhite.

Mrs Timms looked up from ministering to Martha's two small brothers and said, 'I don't know as I like you being up there so much, Martha. We don't know what you're up to, do we? And I don't doubt it's damp there, with those old stone floors. You could catch your death of cold, in that thin frock.'

'It's not that damp, Mum, honest,' said Martha. 'And William's up there too,' she added, with an un-Martha-like touch of cunning.

'Ah,' said Mrs Timms, a little mollified. She considered William a sensible boy.

'Schoolmaster's boy?' said Mr Timms, cutting himself a hunk of bread. 'Nice lad. Got a civil tongue in his head – time to give you a "Good morning" and that. Not like some I could name.'

'It's funny he's still got time for you and Susie,' said Mrs Timms. 'Boys that age usually like to be off with each other, not with girls.'

Martha said, 'He doesn't like the other boys that much. He doesn't like what they do – just fighting and mucking about. He likes doing things with us.'

'Such as?' said Mr Timms, lighting his pipe and pulling up a chair for his feet. He looked all set for a long chat.

'Oh, just things,' said Martha hastily, getting down from the table. She wasn't keen on too many questions just at that moment, never having been good at concealment. 'You can read our Martha like a book,' her mother used to say. It would be safer to beat a hasty retreat.

'Shall I have my bath, Mum?' she said.

'Yes dear, if you like,' said her mother, faintly surprised.

Martha climbed the narrow, creaky stairs of the cottage. Outside, the sky was darkening a little, and the birds were noisy. Night was not far off. Martha sighed, and thought to herself: 'I bet it's going to be a bad one.' The afternoon's events were still with her, circling around uncomfortably somewhere in the back of her thoughts, and in any case she led a dreadful night-life, haunted by nameless fears that pursued her into bed and then harried her in the form of dreams. Her nights were peopled with all the stuff of fairy-tales – witches, goblins, giants – and other, vaguer horrors, that rose up, grinning, to confront her as she wandered in familiar places and then hunted her through strange landscapes as she fled, sobbing, only to wake up in the nick of time to find herself lying in her own bed. And even then she would lie unreassured until she had followed a private ritual. Before she could be certain that she was back in real life, and not still part of her own dream, she must get up, creep over the cold lino to the door, and grope her way across the darkened landing to her parents' bedroom. There, opening the door quietly so as not to wake them, she would stand for a moment and stare at the shapes of their bodies under the bedclothes and listen to the comfortable sound of their breathing. And then, at last, it would be all right and she could go back to bed reassured. She never woke her parents: reason told her that there was little they could do to help in any case. The nights were something she must endure alone.

William and Susie did not suffer in the same way. William, when he dreamed at all, dreamed adventures, he said. 'Like in old films on the telly. And it's always me who's the captain or whatever. Smashing.'

Susie did not dream. 'Except,' she had admitted reluctantly, 'when I've ate too much, and then it's more a stomach ache than a dream.'

Martha woke up in the middle of the night, feeling cold again. She had not been dreaming, and decided that a storm must have woken her, though everything was quiet now, and there was a pale light in the room from the moon outside. She was just going to turn over and go to sleep again when something over in the far side of the room, beside the wardrobe, caught her eye. There was a shadow on the floor, and she had the impression that just before she looked at it, it had moved. It was half on the floor now, and half going up the wall, and the part of it on the wall, had, very clearly, the shape of a figure in a cloak, with a hooded head widening out into shoulders and a humped back.

It's the curtain, she thought, and she reached out a hand and twitched the curtain at the window. But the shadow did not twitch in return. She shot back under the bedclothes again, her heart thumping.

'She will be looking for your weaknesses . . .'

'Oh no she won't,' thought Martha with sudden resolution. 'Not shadows on the wall, and things under the bed and inside cupboards. I got over all that sort of thing years ago. She won't get me that way.'

Very quickly, in case her courage should suddenly collapse, she scrambled out of bed and shot over to the door and snapped on the electric light, her eyes on the shadow all the time. The room was instantly filled with harsh yellow light, penetrating every corner and defining every uncertainty. The shadow vanished too, but it did not vanish until a second or so after Martha had pressed down the switch. It had been there for an instant after the light came on.

She got back into bed, leaving the light on, and pulled the bedclothes up to her chin. Much to her own surprise, she did not really feel frightened. 'She was here,' Martha thought, 'at least I'm pretty sure she was. But I beat her.' With the light still on, she turned round and went to sleep again.

William, leaning up against the churchyard wall watching the village go about its early-morning business, saw Martha come up the lane from her home and turn towards the shop. He was waiting for her, but he gave no sign, and Martha in her turn, went into the shop without indicating that she had seen him. It was a private arrangement. The girls understood that William felt faintly bothered by the fact that he preferred to play with them rather than with Ron at the garage, or the Sadler boys, or indeed any of the other boys, and that the price they must pay for his company was to be discreet about it. Even Susie, usually so blunt and outspoken, respected this. She needed William: they would argue for hours, trying to get the better of each other, but they shared the same enthusiasms and ideas. They were both purposeful, deliberate, impatient of time-wasting. They always had a scheme in hand, a plan to be carried out. William generated ideas, Susie provided the practical suggestions. Today, for instance, they were going to start making a sledge for the winter. Thinking ahead, that was. Susie was supposed to be bringing some nails and a hammer from her father's work-bench, and they already had some wood up there.

William screwed his eyes up in the sunshine, staring at the door of the shop to see if Martha had got hold of Susie yet. He remembered that old lady they'd met up at the barn yesterday: she'd been a bit funny. Nice, but funny. All that stuff she'd told them about a witch: if anybody else went on like that you'd think they were barmy, but somehow with her you didn't. Martha had got quite scared, but then Martha was like that. You couldn't blame her, it was just the way she was made, and she was all right really, old Martha. He began to whistle through the gap in his teeth. 'Come on, for goodness' sake, can't you.'

Martha pushed the shop door, and it opened with a decisive ping. She sometimes thought that when she was an old lady she'd remember every detail of Mrs Poulter's shop and where everything was kept: the bootlaces and drawing-pins in the box under the dishcloths; the faded brown postcards of the village in the drawer under the till; the sticks of liquorice behind the tins of soup. And behind the counter, Mrs Poulter, a larger, plumper edition of Susie, with her hair piled up on top of her head and eyes that missed nothing. She was like a spider, Martha thought, sitting in the middle of her web with fingers on strands reaching out all over the village like telegraph wires keeping her supplied with information. She could talk, listen to gossip, slice bacon and count change all at once, without pausing for breath. And Susie would be beside her, often as not, watching and listening, prompting her mother from time to time if she forgot a name or an item of information. She was there now, sorting change in the till, one ear cocked towards her mother.

'Mrs Fox up the hill had another boy,' said Mrs Poulter. 'That's three in a row – she won't be best pleased. And the Salter boy come banging on the door at ten o'clock last night if you please, could he use the phone 'cos the box was out of order again. I mean, I ask you! Susie, there's Martha come for you. So I said just this once, and I mean just this once. That's two and three, dear, eggs is up threepence this week, I'm afraid.'

'I'm off, Mum,' said Susie, wriggling under the counter.

'Mind you're not late for your dinner. I hear old Mr Harrison's poorly again. Nurse was up there this morning . . .'

The two girls stepped out into the street, the door closing behind them and cutting Mrs Poulter off in full flow. It was a bright morning after the storm, very clear, so that from the rise in the road beyond the shop you could see quite a long way across the countryside with the trees and hedges dark green, almost black, against the bleached cornfields. The long line of the hill stretched out slackly against the pale blue sky and high above the valley larks hung quivering, as though suspended by invisible strings. As they passed the churchyard William fell in beside them.

'You got those nails, Susie?'

Susie patted the bulging pocket of her jeans complacently. 'I always remember things, don't I?'

As they walked up to the barn, Martha told them what had happened to her in the night.

Susie scoffed. 'You're a right nit, Martha, you are. It was a nightmare, that's all.'

'It wasn't,' said Martha obstinately. 'I know about nightmares, don't I? This was different.'

'How long did it stay after you put the light on,' asked William. 'One second? Two?'

'About that. I didn't actually count. But long enough to be sure.'

Susie sniffed, stumping ahead of them across the field. The barn lay in the sunshine, the shape of it melting into the shape of the land as though it had not been built there but had simply grown. The wavy roof was bright gold with lichen: in winter it would turn emerald green.

Inside the barn everything was quite ordinary, cool and quiet. 'Let's have those nails,' said William.

Susie disgorged the nails from her pocket.

'And the hammer.'

'You never said anything about a hammer.'

'I did.'

'You did not, William Harris.'

William opened his mouth to argue further, and then a little grey cloud of doubt crept into his head.

27

Maybe it was he who said he would provide a hammer.

'Bother,' he said irritably. 'Now we can't do the sledge.' He looked with regret at the pile of wood, fresh, uncut, crying out for attention. Nearly two weeks it had taken to get that lot, one way and another.

'No use crying over spilt milk,' said Susie. 'You shouldn't have forgot the hammer. We'll have to do something else.'

Martha had never been all that keen on the sledge. Carpentry was the kind of thing she got left out of, being no good with her hands. Now she said quickly, 'Couldn't we get those ropes up over the rafter again and swing on them.'

'OK. Get the end and chuck it up over the beam. I'll catch it. No, higher than that, stupid. Here, let me.'

Finally they had the rope fixed up and securely

knotted. William tugged it a few times to test it. 'Strong enough. We ought to put some hay underneath, though, in case we slip. This floor's jolly hard.'

There was a pile of hay in the far corner. Susie went over to fetch some. She stooped over the heap to pick it up and then suddenly jumped backwards with a yell.

'What's up?' said William.

'Something moved under there,' said Susie, showing a great deal more emotion than was usual for her.

'Mouse,' said William.

'No. Bigger than that. You can get it yourself. I'm not going near that hay again.'

William moved across the barn floor and stood looking at the hay. It was thick, old and dusty. He poked it with his foot, and the whole of one end of the pile heaved slightly.

They all three raced for the door.

'Crumbs!' said William. 'There really is something!'

'Now do you believe me?' said Martha triumphantly. 'About what happened in the night?'

'Doesn't follow,' said Susie. 'This might be something quite different. I bet it is, too.'

They stood in the doorway, watching the hay, prepared for instant flight. Nothing at all happened. William picked up a slate that had fallen from the roof and threw it at the hay. It landed with a soft thud, and still nothing happened. But it was dark in that corner, and difficult to see well from where they were.

'Oh, look,' said William, 'maybe we imagined it. It's your fault, Martha, you've made us all jumpy.' He began to walk back into the barn, with the girls behind him.

Six yards from the hay they stopped. William searched the floor and found a pebble, which he tossed into the heap. And then, very slowly, it heaved again. They stared, fascinated, and as they stared something began to emerge from one end, sliding out over the flagstones, making a slight rasping noise.

It was dark, thick, round and scaly, tapering to a point. And it had a foot attached to it, huge and webbed, with claws.

They were frozen to the spot. Susie said in a voice that was not her own, 'It's some sort of enormous lizard thing.' Martha could not have spoken to save her life.

And then suddenly William said, 'Look! Look at the other end!'

Smoke was filtering up through the hay, and as they looked a crisp little flame licked up, and another.

'Water!' yelled William. 'Quick! From the tap out-side. Get that old bucket, Susie. I'll fill the drinking-trough.'

It seemed to take minutes to get the water. When they got back the whole of one end of the hay was smouldering, and the scaly tail twitched contentedly on the flagstones. Martha thought she saw the outline of a great head under the hay, and shut her eyes in horror.

William and Susie hurled the water at it. There was a hissing sound, and the tail thrashed. But the flames shot up again. William looked round frantically, and then he dashed outside.

It took him nearly a minute to wrench the old fire extinguisher off the wall outside. It had been there so long that the holder was all rusted up. It's probably so old it's useless, he thought despairingly. He knew all too well what to do: he'd read the instructions often enough, in idle moments – 'In case of emergency re-move from holder and bang nozzle on the ground.' He lifted the thing up – it seemed terribly heavy – and brought the sharp end down on the ground with a crash. Immediately a thick stream of white, foamy liquid gushed out. Staggering under the weight, he lifted it again and directed it at the hay.

The thing writhed wildly. Clouds of thick black smoke poured up, making them all cough, and the white liquid gushed everywhere, all over the hay and the floor. There was a horrible smell, and the whole barn was filled with a shrill hissing noise. William was spluttering and coughing as he tried to get the extinguisher nearer and nearer to the hay. He could hardly see a thing.

Suddenly the stream of white stuff faltered, and then

stopped altogether. He dropped the extinguisher and they all retreated to the door, choking.

Gradually the smoke cleared. They peered anxiously into the barn. There was a tide of white stuff over the floor, but where the hay had been was a blackened mess, and nothing else. They approached cautiously, and William poked it with a stick. A lot of the hay had been burnt, and what was left concealed nothing at all. Paddling in the mess, he spread it around the floor to make sure. There was absolutely nothing there.

'There!' said Martha. 'Just like last night! Afterwards you think it can't have happened, but this time we all saw. Not just me. You were *brave*, William.'

William, slightly dazed, was still poking about in the hay. 'Actually, I didn't really stop to think,' he said, with a quick glance at Susie to see how she was taking it. 'I just kind of bashed it and hoped it wouldn't bash me back.'

Susie's round, pink face was quite pale. 'You've probably done the best thing,' she said grudgingly. 'Anyway it got rid of it. Now what are we going to do? We'll have to do something about this mess, or tell someone.'

'We ought to tell Miss Hepplewhite,' said Martha.

Susie looked doubtful. 'I dunno,' she said. 'Look, if we go and tell her that there was a great scaly thing under the hay and it breathed smoke and set it on fire, and now there's nothing there, d'you really think she's going to believe us?'

'Yes,' said Martha simply.

They had never before opened the door in the wall that led through into Miss Hepplewhite's garden, and it seemed presumptuous to do so now. And yet they all felt that there had, yesterday, been an unspoken invitation. Inside there was a big garden, with lawns and flower-beds and shrubberies full of unkempt, sprawling plants, and little paths leading away to other, wilder places. The house was large, square and stolid, with tall windows that matched each other and fingers of ivy reaching up to the roof. The woodwork needed painting and there were patches on the walls where the plaster had peeled off.

Miss Hepplewhite was cutting roses and laying them in a shallow basket. She wore a huge straw hat, tied under her chin with some kind of veiling and adorned with strange wax fruits and flowers made of material. Martha stared at it with fascination.

'I'm sorry to bother you,' said William, clearing his throat awkwardly, 'but I'm afraid we have to tell you something.'

'Are you bothering me?' said Miss Hepplewhite, a little sharply. 'Perhaps I am the best judge of that. Well, I take it she has come?'

They looked at each other, all reluctant to tell the story. At last William spoke, with Martha adding her bit about the events of the night.

'I'm sorry about the mess in the barn,' he finished.

'I'll have it seen to,' said Miss Hepplewhite carelessly. Beckoning them to follow, she led the way up to a terrace in front of the house and sat down in a basket chair. The children sat down beside her.

'We can talk better here,' said Miss Hepplewhite, fanning herself with her hat. 'I must say I don't think much of her opening effort. Elementary stuff. She has underestimated you, if I may say so.' She looked at them with approval and Martha felt a warm glow creep over her. Somehow Miss Hepplewhite's good opinion seemed very important.

'Was it all right about the fire extinguisher?' asked William anxiously.

'An inspiration. Exactly the right tactics. You took her by surprise. The important thing is never to meet her on her own ground. One must surprise her.'

'You mean,' said William, 'that if I'd – well, charged it with a lance or something – then she might have won?'

'Very likely,' said Miss Hepplewhite. 'You must never play the game according to her rules. The one weapon we have against her, apart from disbelief, is reason. And she knows very little about science. She has a strong dislike for the laws of nature: she is always trying to go against them. Our strength is to use them against her.'

'Must we keep calling her "Her"?' asked Martha.

'No,' said Miss Hepplewhite. 'It is inconvenient, I agree. We will call her Morgan. I have always thought that one of her most convincing parts.'

'Do you think we've got rid of her?' asked Susie.

Miss Hepplewhite stared out across the roses. Bees hummed, and somewhere in the chestnut trees behind them a wood-pigeon rumbled contentedly. 'I doubt it,' she said at last. 'She is not usually so easily routed. But you've made a good start. Maybe we should follow up the advantage.'

'How?' said William.

'Well, there's something to be said for the time-honoured methods. She respects them. We could have a Walpurgis Night.'

'A what?'

'An old ritual for the expulsion of witches. Noise is the important element. It was done in villages in the old days on the eve of May Day to drive out evil spirits for the forthcoming year. The people marched through the streets making as much noise as possible with bells, shotguns, gongs – anything they could lay hands on. And burning bundles of particular herbs – hemlock, spurge, and rosemary in particular, if I remember rightly.'

'We'd have to do it round the barn, then?' said William.

'Precisely. It should really be in the evening. Would your parents be likely to give permission for an evening outing?'

The children looked at each other doubtfully.

'Perhaps a personal note,' said Miss Hepplewhite with cunning, 'inviting you to take tea with me. We will not mention the Walpurgis activities.'

'That'll do, I reckon,' said Susie. 'Mum likes getting letters.'

Miss Hepplewhite led them inside the house. It seemed enormous. Rooms led one from another. Flights of stone steps tumbled away into long, gloomy passages. It smelt of flowers, leather, and old newspapers.

'It's a big house,' ventured Martha.

'Too big,' said Miss Hepplewhite, sitting down at a desk. 'I rattle about in it like a pea in a pod. Once there were lots of us, when I was a girl. Children everywhere, and noise, and people coming and going. Now there is only me.' She began to write, in clear, sloping hand-writing with very black ink.

'How old are you?' asked Martha.

The others looked shocked. 'That's rude, Martha,' whispered Susie.

But Miss Hepplewhite did not seem in the least put out. She went on writing as she answered. 'Around eighty. I shall be no more precise than that. In any case I have reached a stage when give or take a year or two makes little difference, odd as that may seem to you.' She signed the first note with a flourish and put it in an envelope. When all three were written she handed them to the children. 'I shall expect you shortly after dusk. Do you have guns?'

They were taken aback. Susie and Martha shook their heads. 'I've a pop-gun,' said William.

'Bring it, then.'

'She writes a lovely hand,' said Mrs Poulter, reading the letter for the third time. ' "Yours very sincerely, Letitia Hepplewhite". There's a nice old-fashioned name, Letitia.'

'Is it all right, then, Mum?' said Susie, her mouth full of baked beans.

'I suppose so. I wouldn't mind having a look round up there myself. I don't doubt she's got some nice things. Maybe I'll walk up with you.'

'No!' said Susie violently.

'All right, suit yourself,' said her mother, offended. There was a pause. Then Mrs Poulter said, in an offhand way, 'Posh, is it, up there?'

Susie helped herself to another slice of bread. 'Quite,' she said, with a sidelong glance at her mother. She sensed an advantage and decided to sit on it for a while. You never knew when it might come in handy.

Martha's mother, always practical, said, 'Well, if you're getting tea up there you won't want another one down here, will you?'

William's father, surfacing momentarily from a sea of O-level exam scripts, read the letter and merely grunted. 'She must be out of her mind,' he said, 'inviting you lot to tea.'

William said, 'As a matter of fact, she likes us.' But his father had already gone back to the exam papers.

It was almost dusk when they set off for the barn. The countryside was very dark and quiet under a sky that had turned from pale turquoise to a deep midnight blue. In the village, lights were coming on in the windows, and they could see the grey flicker of television screens. The lights of cars dipped and wavered along the road. In the field they were back in an older, more unpredictable world: there were little rushing noises in the hedge and sudden panic-stricken flutterings as birds fled to safety. There was a feeling of things watching, and waking, and Martha kept close behind William and the torch.

Miss Hepplewhite was already at the barn, surrounded by a strange assortment of dinner bells, an enormous oriental-looking gong, and a pile of saucepans and firearms. She had also provided several bundles of leaves and branches, which were set fire to and strewn about in front of the barn. They were rather green and refused to burn properly, but they smoked away on the ground and gave out a strong, herby smell. She instructed the children to help themselves, and set to and make as much noise as possible. At first they felt positively inhibited. Martha couldn't remember ever having been told before to *make* a noise. But after a while they began to enjoy themselves. Susie rushed up and down, howling like a wolf and banging the gong, which made a tremendous hollow noise. Martha, a dinner bell in each hand, discovered a very effective high-pitched shriek. William, making

Indian war-cries, alternated between his pop-gun and two saucepan lids banged together. Miss Hepplewhite stood at the door of the barn watching with satisfaction.

At last they collapsed on the ground, exhausted.

'I can't hardly speak,' said Susie, 'my throat's that sore.'

'It was a most impressive performance,' said Miss Hepplewhite. 'I don't think she will have liked that at all.'

'Do you think it's done the trick?' asked William.

Miss Hepplewhite looked round. The sudden silence, after all the noise, was like something you could reach out and touch. It was almost dark, with the sky only a shade paler than the ground, and William's torch throwing a long yellow light across the cobbles. In the bushes a blackbird suddenly chattered, and was silent.

'We shall have to wait and see,' said Miss Hepplewhite. 'And now what about something to eat?'

Three

The days passed, and things were peaceful up at the barn. To begin with, they kept glancing round anxiously. They had been caught out once: next time they would be on their guard. But nothing happened. Piles of hay remained piles of hay. Nothing whisked across the floor but field-mice, and the shadow that sometimes drifted above their heads from rafter to rafter was just the old owl who had made his home in the barn.

'I reckon we scared her off,' said Susie.

Martha crossed her fingers behind her back, where the others couldn't see, just to be on the safe side.

'You know something?' said William. 'We ought to ask Miss Hepplewhite to tea. It would be polite – I mean, she had us. And she's nice.'

Susie considered. 'Where?' she asked.

'Here. In the barn.'

'But it's her barn. We can't say "Would you like to come and have tea with us in your own barn", can we?'

'Yes we can. She'll understand. There's nowhere else, anyway. We'll tidy it up.'

Susie looked round. 'There's no table. Or chairs. Or tablecloth.'

'Who wants a tablecloth?' said William with scorn. 'It's the food that's important.'

'I like to do things proper,' said Susie.

Martha said coaxingly, 'Oh, come on, Susie, don't spoil it. We could make it ever so nice – pick flowers and put them in jam-jars. And we could bring food from home. You could get a lot from the shop.'

'Mum's got some of those tins of little sausages,' said Susie, tempted. 'The ones you eat off little sticks. I reckon as I could borrow one without her noticing.'

'Jolly good,' said William. 'And we'll want crisps, too, and nuts. We'll make it a different sort of tea from hers, for a change.'

It was. Miss Hepplewhite's tea had been cucumber sandwiches, cut very thin, and china tea from a silver pot, and tiny pink and white sugared cakes, and buttered scones. Theirs was bars of chocolate, peanuts, crisps, sausages, and ginger beer. Susie also took a paper tablecloth and napkins from the shop, which she spread over a packing-case.

'There,' she said, satisfied. 'Now it looks posh. Like when Mum does the Women's Institute teas in the church hall.'

'It's a nosh-up,' said William, 'not a Women's Institute tea.'

Susie glared.

Miss Hepplewhite was a most appreciative guest. She rose magnificently to the occasion and arrived wearing a long silk dress that whispered as she walked, and many brooches and rings, and an immense hat, decorated beyond belief. The girls stared at it admiringly.

'That's lovely,' said Susie. 'My mum would love that. She's keen on hats. She buys a new one every spring.'

'Foolish!' said Miss Hepplewhite. 'Extravagant! My hats are all over twenty years old. A hat should be treasured and allowed to mature. This one belonged to my mother.'

She particularly liked the crisps. 'Delicious. Quite

delicious. A most unusual taste. Where do you get them?'

'From our shop,' said Susie, surprised. 'I'm not being rude, but it does seem funny to have got to be as old as you and never eaten crisps before.'

'I've led a sheltered life,' said Miss Hepplewhite, licking her fingers delicately. 'Tell me, do you think your mother would deliver me some, twice weekly?'

You bet she would, thought Susie. She'd bring them herself. But she had already decided not to share Miss Hepplewhite, at any rate for the time being.

'I'll bring them,' she said firmly.

Back at the shop, later that afternoon, Susie stood by her mother behind the counter and wondered idly if Miss Hepplewhite would care to try a sherbert stick sometime: she might not know about those either. It had been a most satisfactory tea-party. Miss Hepplewhite had proved to have what Susie felt to be a proper respect for food – indeed, she had eaten more sausages than any of them. And afterwards she had told them stories of her own childhood, and what the village had been like in old-fashioned times. It had been enthralling. She talks lovely, Susie thought to herself, like a book – with commas and full-stops and no 'ums' and 'ahs' when she can't think how to put things. And she talks to you like you were grown-ups, leaving in the long words.

Lost in her thoughts, she jumped as her mother suddenly tapped her on the shoulder. 'You asleep or something, Susie? I said pass me a bag for Mrs Slater's apples.'

Susie tugged a paper bag off the bunch that hung under the counter and returned to present-day Steeple

Hampden. Mrs Poulter was talking of the new motor-way that was to be built on the far side of Chipping Ledbury, the market town a few miles from the village. 'It won't do us no harm, speaking personally,' said Mrs Poulter. 'My turnover should go up. I'm thinking of a bigger ice-cream cabinet. We might get some of those American tourists coming to the village. I might even do teas,' she added dreamily, 'out the back. With some of those nice striped umbrellas.'

'We don't want to get like Bourton, do we?' said her customer. 'Or Burford. Full of cars and people in the summer so you can't hear yourself think?'

'I daresay not,' said Mrs Poulter, with a trace of regret. 'You know,' she went on, 'they say at one time it were to come right through the valley, that motor-way. Right through! Six lanes, and all those bridges and tunnels and all.'

'Never!'

'That's what they say. And then they changed their minds and thought they'd put it over the other side of Chipping, at Banton, where that big factory is. It'll have to go, that factory, but they say that Mr Steel as owns it will get near a hundred thousand pounds compensation for it. To them that hath shall be given, isn't it? That'll be five and eleven, Mrs Slater.'

'Well, it's a good thing for us, anyway. A motorway through the Sharnbrook valley! I hope I never live to see the day.'

It was closing time. Susie helped her mother tidy the counter, put the cover over the till and pull down the blinds. Then they went through to the back.

Susie switched on the television and lay down on her stomach in front of it, waiting for the picture to come on. After a few seconds, the sound came, but the screen merely showed what appeared to be an unending shower of white rain. She got up and fiddled with the knobs, but the white rain continued.

'Mum! There's something wrong with the telly.'

Mrs Poulter came and fiddled unsuccessfully. 'If it's the tube ...' she said darkly. 'Thirty bob I paid last time we had the man to it.'

Susie got up. 'I'm going round to Martha's,' she said.

She let herself out of the back door and walked round

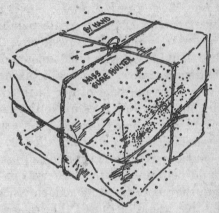

the shop and up the path at the side. Glancing at the shop door to see if she had remembered to turn round the 'OPEN' sign, she saw something on the step. A square brown paper parcel. Bending down to look at it she was surprised to find that it was addressed, in large clear letters written with a black felt pen, to Miss Susie Poulter. The same pen had written 'By Hand', in one corner, and underlined it.

Susie sat down on the step and tore the string off, and then the paper. Inside was a white cardboard box. She took the lid off.

It was a cake. A large, round cake, most exquisitely

iced and decorated. Susie had never seen anything like it. The icing was white, smooth and glistening, with rows of swirls and rosettes round the edge, and the lettering was pink, delicate and looping. It said 'To dear Susie, with love'.

'It's not my birthday,' thought Susie, confused. 'Who on earth . . . ?' She hunted in the box for a card or letter, but there was nothing.

Could it be her mother? A surprise, for some mysterious reason? Susie cast a shrewd eye over the cake and decided that an elaborate confection like that couldn't have cost a penny under twenty-five shillings. Her mother would never spend that amount of money without letting her know. No, it was someone else. A relation, who'd got the date of her birthday wrong. Aunt Pam? But Aunt Pam lived in Nottingham: how could she get a parcel here by hand? She sat staring at the cake, puzzling. Then she picked the box up, very carefully, and began to carry it indoors to see if her mother could help unravel the mystery. But halfway up the path she stopped, with a sudden vision of the commotion that would be caused. The cake would no longer be hers, that was certain. It would be taken over by her mother and she might get a slice for supper at the very most. And it had been addressed most firmly to her, and it said 'To dear Susie, with love'. It suddenly occurred to her that they could have the most wonderful feast with it up at the barn. And she would cut it and she would dispense it. She decided to take it with her to Martha's, and maybe show it to Martha. She put the lid back on the box and carefully wrapped it up again.

Martha was swinging on the farmyard gate. Behind her the cows stood nose to tail, waiting to be milked, swishing and blowing gently in the evening sunshine.

'I want to watch your telly,' said Susie. 'Ours is gone all funny.'

'Has it? So's ours.'

'Let's see,' said Susie, who relied on no one. They went through the farmyard to the cottage and into the kitchen, where Martha's little brothers were playing trains under the table. Martha switched on the television, and the same shower of white rain swam into view. The screen fizzed gently, as though full of silent fireworks.

'It's pretty,' said Martha dreamily. 'You can't tell if the sparks are going upwards or downwards.'

'Don't be daft!' snorted Susie. 'Come on, then, we might as well go out.'

Outside, she produced the parcel from under her arm. 'Here, I've got something to show you.' She opened the box.

Martha was gratifyingly impressed. She said, 'Oh!' and 'Goodness!' and 'You are *lucky*, Susie.' And finally, 'Who gave it to you?'

'I don't know,' said Susie.

Martha stared. A present like that didn't usually arrive quite anonymously.

'I really don't. There wasn't any card or nothing like that. And no postmark because it came by hand. I thought we'd eat it up at the barn tomorrow.'

Martha's eyes grew yet wider. 'That'd be nice, Susie.'

Susie looked lovingly at the cake. 'Wouldn't do any harm to try a bit now, would it?'

'I could get a knife from the kitchen,' offered Martha.

She was back in a few minutes. Carefully, to wreck the beautiful design as little as possible, Susie cut two

thin slices. She levered the first one out with the knife and passed it to Martha balanced on the blade, as she had seen her mother do. But her hand shook slightly and the slice toppled and rolled off onto the grass, where it lay on its side.

'Sorry,' she said. Martha picked it up and opened her mouth to take a bite, when Susie said in a queer voice, 'Stop a minute. Look there!'

Martha shut her mouth, cake in hand, and looked. Where the slice had lain on the grass there was a scar, like the burn left by a bonfire, and the blades of grass were still bending and shrinking. Martha gasped and dropped the slice of cake: her fingers, where she had held it, were pink and wrinkled as though she had burned herself on a pan.

'Susie – there's something wrong with it!'

Susie bent over the cake and sniffed. It smelt, not of sugar, but faintly sulphurous, with a whiff of ammonia. She jumped up and fetched a stick from the hedge. Lifting it up high, she jabbed it down furiously right into the exquisite centre of the cake. There was a hissing noise and a hideous smell, and then, where the cake had been, nothing but a circle of scorched grass.

The girls stared in horror. 'We nearly ate it!' said Susie. 'Our insides might have been like that!'

A terrible chill stole over them. Their limbs became leaden, and cold trickled down their spines. The sky seemed to grow darker, and the ordinary, familiar hedges loomed dangerously. There was a heaviness in the air, as before a thunderstorm. Martha looked at Susie, and Susie shifted uneasily. 'It was her, wasn't it?' said Susie in a whisper, and Martha nodded. Without another word they got up and hurried away. A smell of sulphur hung all about.

They ran into Martha's house.

'What's wrong with you two?' asked her mother. 'You look like you'd seen a ghost.'

Martha was still shuddering, but Susie had begun to recover herself. 'It's raining,' she said, 'that's all.'

The television was on. Martha's mother, seeing them look towards it, said, 'Funny, isn't it – it came all right as soon as you'd gone out.'

They sat down in front of it, and the room was quiet except for soothing voices from the screen, and, for Martha, the thumping of her own heart.

The next day they told Miss Hepplewhite about the

47

cake. She was contemptuous: so much so that Susie and Martha could not bring themselves to admit how near they had come to eating it. The thought still made them shudder.

'Really! The most elementary stuff!' said Miss Hepplewhite. 'She is treating you like children in a fairy story. So long as she goes on like this I really do not think we have much to worry about.'

'It's making me nervous,' said Susie petulantly. 'I don't know where I am any more.' She pulled her plait round to the front and began to chew the end of it, a sure sign that she was feeling disturbed.

'Ah,' said Miss Hepplewhite, 'that is just her intention. To be unsettling. But you must resist her – I'm sure you have the resources. You don't seem to me the kind of person to be easily rattled.'

Susie dropped the plait and went pink. A pleased smile crept across her face. They were sitting in Miss Hepplewhite's garden. Great blowsy roses sagged in the sunshine and dropped their petals on the ground. A tabby cat rolled ecstatically in the catmint and overhead rooks slid lazily down the aircurrents and swirled above the chestnuts behind the house.

'Could you tell us more about those old-fashioned times?' asked Martha. Susie edged a little closer to Miss Hepplewhite's chair.

'Dear me,' said Miss Hepplewhite, 'how odd that you should find it interesting. What more can I tell you, I wonder? Did I mention that I was one of the first people in the village to ride a bicycle? I was thought most dashing – everyone used to stand in their doorways and watch.'

'What did you wear,' asked Susie, 'when you were our age?'

'Oh, none of the nice convenient clothes you have. Holland dresses, with white frilly pinafores on top, and long buttoned boots. One had to do each button up individually with a button-hook, and the hairs on one's legs would get caught up in them and sting most unpleasantly.'

Martha felt her legs tingling in sympathy.

'What about boys?' said William. 'What did they do, I mean?'

'Oh, life for boys was very similar to nowadays. My brothers spent their time falling out of trees and fishing in the Sharnbrook, much as you do. Less exacting standards of behaviour were set for them. "Boys will be boys," my mother used to say, in that rather irritating phrase. I always used to think girls should be allowed to be girls too.'

'There isn't so much difference nowadays,' said Susie. William snorted indignantly.

'Mind, we led a pampered life compared to most of the village children,' Miss Hepplewhite went on. 'Most children left school at twelve or so in those days and were set to work. Stone-picking in the fields, helping with the harvest, haymaking, and sheep-shearing or just helping out in the home. It was a hard life for most in those days, working the year through just to make ends meet, and never a holiday in their lives. Few people ever left the village then even to go to Chipping Ledbury, or Oxford. No cars or buses. No television. Ah well, times change. Frequently for the better, I suspect.' Miss Hepplewhite sighed, tipping her straw hat forward a little to keep the sun out of her eyes: her face was a delicate tracery of wrinkles in fine, old skin.

'Must have been funny without a telly,' said Susie.

'Seems funny now without it,' said William. 'Ours

has bust again. Least it has whenever I want to look at it.'

The girls stared at him. 'Does it look as though it's full of white rain?' asked Martha.

'Yes. That's it.'

'So does ours,' said Susie. 'And Martha's.'

They all looked at Miss Hepplewhite, who said sharply, 'What's that?'

'All our televisions have gone wrong in the same way,' said William. 'Do you think it could be ... ?'

Miss Hepplewhite pondered, frowning. 'How do they work, these instruments?'

'Well,' said William importantly, 'it's all a question of sound waves, you see ...'

'I thought it was a picture,' said Miss Hepplewhite.

'Well, yes, it is, but it's still waves, you see, going through the air, and getting – kind of – well, pinned down – in, er, in television sets.'

Miss Hepplewhite looked at him enquiringly. 'It's not absolutely clear to me yet,' she said with great courtesy.

'It's vibrations in the air, and sort of – er – currents and things.' A pause. 'Matter of fact,' said William, 'I'm not quite sure how they *do* work.'

'Mmm,' said Miss Hepplewhite. She looked troubled. 'Do they often go wrong?'

'Yes,' said Susie and Martha.

'Ours doesn't,' said William. 'It's almost new. And anyway, it's funny it should be all of them at once.'

'If it *is* anything to do with her,' said Miss Hepplewhite, 'then it is definitely cause for concern. It means she is moving onto our ground, and into our time. It could make her more difficult to deal with altogether. Tell me, is anything else necessary to receive these pictures apart from the box with the window in the front?'

'There's the aerial,' said William.

'Aerial?'

William explained. He arranged sticks on the ground in the shape of a television aerial.

'Ah!' said Miss Hepplewhite. 'Those things. My natural curiosity is failing me in my old age. I have often seen them but never bothered to enquire as to their function. I took them for some kind of lightning conductor. Rooftops fairly bristle with them nowadays – to the uninitiated they might well appear to have some kind of ritual significance. Like the elder or rowan over the door in older times.'

'What was that for?' asked Martha.

'General protection against witchcraft. Now I wonder ... Morgan is notoriously unreceptive to new ideas. It may be that she has quite mistaken the significance of this television: she may think it altogether more central to our lives than it really is. An understandable mistake, after all, in one accustomed to a long tradition of worship of one kind or another.'

The children looked puzzled. 'I'm sorry,' said Susie, 'I don't really understand.'

'Well,' said Miss Hepplewhite, 'consider the evening scene in your home, and millions of other homes.'

They considered. The circle of chairs, all turned to face the luminous square of the set, the respectful silence, save for the confident murmurings from the box ...

'Oh!' said William, 'I get it! She thinks it's some kind of god!'

'Quite possibly. In which case we can disregard this particular move of hers. It cannot harm us.'

*　　　*　　　*

Nevertheless, it was tiresome. For several days the televisions fizzed and spat whenever the children approached them: mysteriously, they righted themselves whenever they were not there. They had to endure a great deal of unjust accusation.

'You've had the back off of it, Susie,' said Mrs Poulter angrily.

'I have not. I never touched it.'

'Then you've got a jinx on you. It only does it when you're here.'

'Fair enough,' thought Susie, 'I daresay it does.' Resignedly, she went round to find Martha. One could do without the wretched thing for a bit.

William watched a mystified electrician take the set to pieces and put it together again. He nodded, sympathetic, but helpless, when the man said that sometimes you felt there were things in this world that were beyond explanation. 'And I done two years' night school at the Tec on TV repair work,' he added, banging the back into place again.

But later that night William lay awake, uneasy. The creature under the hay had been one thing, but this was quite another. 'If you can see something,' he thought, 'then you can do something about it. Get out and bash it. Even if you're dead scared. But this stuff is creepy. Poisonous cakes that disappear, and spots in television sets. If you told most grown-ups about it they'd just laugh at you, but Miss Hepplewhite doesn't. And she's not daft or anything. As a matter of fact,' he thought, 'she's one of the most un-daft people I've ever met. Which makes it all the creepier.'

Susie had decided to be on her guard. Night and day.

She would take nothing at all on trust. It was infuriating that of the three of them she should be the one who had come nearest to falling victim to Morgan, or whoever this person was. The memory of the cake both annoyed and frightened her. That evening she examined everything most carefully before eating it, and thoroughly searched her room before going to bed. Everything appeared to be in order and the night passed uneventfully.

It was raining dismally in the morning. A skin of water lay on the road outside the shop, with a fine spray lifting off it as the rain continued to stream down, and every passing car sent a small wave rippling up to the step. Clearly it was not a day for going up to the barn: Susie resigned herself to a morning spent in the shop with her mother. Anyway, it wasn't too bad a prospect. She could help herself liberally to the sweets when her mother wasn't looking, and she always enjoyed listening to the to and fro of conversation. You never knew what you might hear: people tended to forget she was there and unburden themselves to her mother, sometimes most interestingly.

For a while things were very quiet. One or two lorry-drivers came in for cigarettes. The bread-man delivered, and Susie had to go out to help him carry in the wire trays of buns and doughnuts. A traveller came, with a new line in cheap stockings: Mrs Poulter examined them critically, and dismissed him.

At ten o'clock Mrs Watts from the pub came in. 'Well, what a day! It's black Friday for us all right, isn't it!'

Mrs Poulter glanced at the window. 'What can you expect? Seems to me it always rains most in August.'

'I'm not talking about the weather,' said Mrs Watts

impatiently. 'I mean the other business. Don't tell me you've not heard!'

Mrs Poulter inclined her head and murmured something noncommittal. Susie knew precisely what her mother was going through. She had heard nothing, but at the same time she could not bring herself to admit it. She, who informed others of what was going on in Steeple Hampden.

'And all because that wretched man's changed his mind. Least, that's what they're saying. It's not right, just because he's got friends in the right places. It's us who's got to suffer. My Tom says he couldn't stand it – he reckons we'll have to move away.'

Mrs Poulter could bear it no longer. 'What's the matter, then?'

'The matter! It's the road, that's what! And after we all thought we were safe. It was on the seven o'clock news this morning. They've changed the route. It's not to go south, where the factory is. They're putting it north after all.'

Mrs Poulter stared. 'Will it be near the village, then?'

'Near! It's to go straight through it!'

Four

As the news spread through the village, there was general consternation. Mrs Poulter had the time of her life, gathering information as people flowed in and out of the shop.

'It's a crying shame, that's what it is. Messing up people's lives just for an old road. Six lanes it'll be, they say. Right slap through the back of the village. There'll be houses pulled down, that's for sure.'

'We'll be shook to bits, all those heavy lorries.'

'Might do you a bit of good, Mrs Poulter,' said someone slyly, 'being as how it would bring more custom.'

'I'm not running one of those motorway caffs,' Mrs Poulter retorted, slapping bacon down onto the counter. 'Lorry-drivers and that. I get a nice type of customer, the way things are, and I don't want any changes.' She seemed to have abandoned her ideas about increased turnover.

Martha's mother said, 'My Tom'll lose his job, when the farm goes. They'll be taking that land, see. I don't know what we'll do.'

'I lived here all my life, and I thought as I'd die here,' said one old lady, who had heard that her cottage would have to go. She looked round helplessly, and the other people in the shop were silent, murmuring sympathetically.

'They'll give you compensation, dear,' said Mrs Poulter, attempting comfort. 'You could maybe get one of those bungalows for old people, over in Chipping.'

'I lived here all my life,' said the old lady again, and Mrs Poulter nodded sadly, silenced.

Susie, who had been quietly absorbing all she heard, said, 'Why's this happened all of a sudden, Mum? I thought you said the road was going through that Mr Steel's factory at Banton?'

Mrs Poulter, temporarily at a loss, looked at her customers for enlightenment.

'Seems he changed his mind,' said the pub-owner's wife. 'They say up to just recent it was all settled, and then all of a sudden he decided he didn't want to lose his factory after all, compensation or not, and he got onto all his important friends – his brother that's a Member of Parliament, and his friends on Chipping Ledbury Council, and his grand friends in London – and they got the plans changed and the road's to go through Steeple Hampden after all.'

'It's a crying shame,' said Mrs Poulter again. 'A lovely valley like this, and a village. Now it wouldn't have done any harm to put it where that factory is. A factory's not a village. It's not got a life of its own. You can have a factory anywhere.'

'They say his wife had something to do with it,' said someone darkly. 'Mr Steel's old now, but he's got this new young wife, and they say she's a regular Madam, and it's what she says goes.'

Susie reported on what she had heard to the others. 'It'll go through our barn, Mum says,' she said disconsolately. 'Then where'll we play?'

William felt anger boil inside him, a protest in the stomach like too many sweets or an unripe apple. Red-faced and shaking with rage, he poured out the story at home and was encouraged as he saw his father, a mild man, gradually infected with his own indignation.

'It's not fair, Dad. They've got no right, have they? It's a kind of bullying, that's what. I mean, why can this Mr Steel and his friends just because they're important fix which way this road goes. So that it mucks us up and not them. It's just not fair.'

'I quite agree, William,' said his father. 'The reason, I'm afraid, is that they know how to go about things the right way, and get reports written, and shown to the right people so that it appears that what they want is the best thing all round.'

'Well, can't we *do* something, Dad?'

'I don't know. I rather doubt it. But we must certainly try. We should at least make a noise about it.'

In the afternoon the clouds had lifted and the rain stopped, leaving a bright, glistening world. The children, knowing that Miss Hepplewhite would not have heard the news, decided that they must go to tell her. William was still bristling like an angry terrier, but Susie, on the surface at least, had reverted to her usual stolid calm. Martha was anxious and jumpy, twitching at noises in the hedgerows and retreating before the pub dog as it came bounding from an alley.

'What's wrong with you?' said Susie. 'You're behaving all funny.'

'I can't help it,' said Martha humbly, 'I feel funny. I think I've got nerves,' she added, remembering a remark of Mrs Poulter's.

They walked slowly through the village. Nearly all the houses and cottages were built of the same stone, an old, worn stone which looks grey on a dull day and turns to bright gold in sunshine. They seemed to grow

one from another, with cottages huddling companion-
ably together, their front doors opening straight onto
the street. Martha walked along with her eyes closed,

thinking: 'I could tell where I was anywhere in the village just from the smells – the lilac in Mrs Lay's garden, and the petrol smell near the garage, and the beer smell at the pub, and the farm smell at home, and apples and bacon in the shop.'

They were passing the high wall round the churchyard now and she could feel the heat coming from the sun-warmed stone. The wall was full of cracks and crannies, with birds popping in and out of them. Sparrows nested deep inside it and if you pressed your ear to the stone you could hear faint cheepings from within. Behind the wall was the churchyard, with gravestones half-buried in high grass. The children sometimes walked among them, reading the inscriptions. Some were so old and worn they were quite illegible, but some had lovely curly writing, all loops and flourishes, and carved cherubs and roses, and names that were the same as people they knew in the village. 'Eliza Lay, beloved wife of John Lay, died 14th April 1789' and 'In Memory of Ebenezer Timms 1774–1836'. High above them soared the spire of the church, black against the sky, with the clouds and the rooks moving around and above it so that if you stared long enough you began to feel as though the whole world was wheeling and spinning and only the spire was still and solid at its centre.

The school playground was still and silent, puddles shining on the empty stretch of tarmac. Through the big windows they could see the desks, neatly ranged, with the chairs pushed up against them, and work the children had done last term still pinned up on the board. Passing the school, they walked along the grass verge beside the road. The hedge brimmed with meadow-sweet, and the dried heads of cow-parsley. Trails of briar hung down, studded with the red fruit of unripe blackberries. It was all very quiet, except for the brushing of their feet in the grass, and the chatter of the birds, and somewhere high above and far away, the drone of an aeroplane.

William said violently, 'I don't want a rotten great road through our valley.'

'None of us do,' said Susie. 'Stands to reason, doesn't it?'

They turned into the field in front of the barn and crossed it in silence. They did not go into the barn but went straight into Miss Hepplewhite's garden through the door in the wall.

She was sitting on the terrace in a basket chair, reading a book. Her straw hat was on the ground beside her and one of her cats sat a little way off, watching a bird and twitching the end of its tail. As the children came up the path she looked up and closed the book. 'Oh dear,' she said, 'I can see from your faces that something has happened. I never saw such a chorus of tragedy. You had better tell me all about it quickly.'

William told her. She listened intently, the wrinkled face expressionless but her eyes very much alert and alive. Once or twice she interrupted with questions.

'You say this is a sudden change of plan? That the motorway should go through the valley?'

'Yes. It's this beastly horrible person called Mr Steel.'

'Ah,' said Miss Hepplewhite thoughtfully, fingering the beads of her necklace.

Martha said in a small voice, 'I think he's been magicked or something. I think it's all something to do with – to do with the other things.'

'Perceptive child,' said Miss Hepplewhite. 'That is undoubtedly the case. It is a catastrophe, I must admit. She has done the unexpected, and moved right onto our ground, where we are at least able to confront her. This time it is she who has made the surprise move.'

Susie's eyes widened, and William said, 'Oh, gosh, it's Morgan, then, is it? Actually I did wonder.'

'I don't get it,' said Susie. 'I mean, why would she want to have a road go right through the barn, and the valley and all, when it's her place, like you said?'

Miss Hepplewhite smoothed her skirt with thin, veined hands. 'It will still be her place, whatever is there. If she holds it then no doubt it will once again become a place of evil. A stretch of road could easily be malevolent – a place where accidents happen.'

The children, sitting round her chair looking up at her, felt suddenly as though something enormous were pressing down on them: a sense of threat and defeat hung all around.

'It's no good telling my dad it's her,' said William. 'He'd just think I'd gone potty or something. Matter of fact, we can't tell anyone, can we?'

'Couldn't we tell this Mr Steel he's been magicked?' said Martha eagerly.

Susie's voice was full of scorn. 'Think he'd believe it? You just going to go up to him, a man with a big house and a factory and lots of cars and all, and say "You know you've been magicked, you have."'

Martha looked away, crushed.

'My dad was going to organize a petition,' said William. 'Not much point now, is there?'

'But of course,' said Miss Hepplewhite briskly. 'It will keep up morale, if nothing else, and give people something to do. At least then they feel they are defending themselves. Meanwhile the real battle lies with us.'

'Us? You mean there's something we can do?'

'Naturally. Unless you intend to let her in without opposition.' Miss Hepplewhite looked round at them with raised eyebrows.

'I should jolly well think not!' said William.

'Good. But whatever we do must be done with the greatest care. Unless I am mistaken she will be here now in person. That is always her last resort, and that is when she is at her most dangerous. And I think too that the time may have come to attack, in which case the initiative will be in your hands. I am too old now for pursuit, as she well knows.'

She is talking as though this wasn't the first time, thought Martha. As though there'd been other times.

She remembered Miss Hepplewhite saying that the barn was far older than her own house – 'She was here long before I came.' Perhaps Miss Hepplewhite was here to deal with Morgan, and that is how she knew so much about what to do.

'Pursuit?' said William, with quickening interest. 'You mean we're going after her?'

'Someone will have to,' said Miss Hepplewhite, 'unless she comes to you. Which is perhaps what we must expect.'

A little wind rustled across the terrace. Below, in the flower-bed, a rose dropped its petals with a silky plop. The cat jumped, and Martha looked round apprehensively.

'What can we do?' asked William. 'I mean, we're not much, are we? Compared to her. Three children.'

'It doesn't matter what you look like or who you are. It's courage and conviction that count,' said Miss Hepplewhite, watching them with a great intensity.

'Well, we've got to, haven't we?' said Susie, in a blunt, almost ill-tempered voice. 'It was us brought her here, with that business in the barn. So it's up to us to get rid of her. Stands to reason.'

She got up, as though the matter was settled, and looked at Martha and William. William nodded, and Martha thought, with a tingle of apprehension: So this is the beginning of things, now. Aloud, she said, 'What do we do if – if she comes?'

'You must find your own weapons,' said Miss Hepplewhite gravely. 'I may not be able to help you when the time comes. Her powers change, and the powers we can use against her change too. Time was when she used to be confounded by the sign of the Cross, but I am afraid that it is losing its power: it has been too much misused. But remember what I have told you before: she cannot abide reason, it runs counter to everything she stands for, and she abominates the laws of nature.'

They left Miss Hepplewhite and began to walk slowly back across the field towards the village. Suddenly Martha said, 'Let's not go back. Let's go up to the Stones.'

'Good idea,' said William. He no longer felt angry, but oddly excited, with a little creep of fear somewhere under the excitement. It's weird, he thought, us being the only ones knowing what's going on. Daft, really, when you come to think of it: I mean, what can *we* do? Aloud, he said, 'Wouldn't it be smashing if we *could* beat her! This Morgan person.'

'It won't be easy,' said Susie, 'with her having these powers. It makes it so nothing's what it seems to be.'

'That's what we've got to remember all the time,' said William. 'We'll have to be crafty. Dead crafty.'

'That's right.' Susie was stumping ahead up the gentle slope of the field, towards the high ground at the side of the valley, William beside her. Martha trailed a pace or two behind.

'You all right?' asked William kindly. 'Not scared or anything?'

'I don't like it,' said Martha, her voice quavering. 'Not knowing what'll happen next. I *am* scared.'

'You mustn't be,' said Susie. 'Bite your nails. Think about something else. Like what's for dinner.'

William said, 'Actually, I like being a bit frightened. It's like going too fast on a sledge. Or climbing a tree and not being quite sure you'll be able to get down.'

Martha was silent. It's all very well for them, she thought, they don't have dreams at night and all that.

Susie doesn't mind lots of things I do: she can pick up spiders and take dead mice out of traps.

They were nearly at the top of the hill now, and the grey shapes of the Hampden Stones were just in sight at the top. Her spirits lifted a little: this was one of her very favourite places.

Steeple Hampden lay in the heart of the Sharnbrook valley. To one side of the village was the Sharnbrook, looping gently through the fields, edged with the blunt heads of willows, spreading their green fans of leaves now in high summer. And beyond the Sharnbrook, on the lower ground where the valley opened out and spread away into the distance, were the jumbled roofs of Chipping Ledbury.

A mile from Steeple Hampden, at the highest point on the low range of hills that formed the side of the valley, stood the Hampden Stones. They were a circle of rough grey stones, dappled with lichen and pock-marked by age, sunk deep in the grass in one corner of a field like old, worn, teeth: a miniature Stonehenge. You could not see them from the village, or from the road, hidden as they were by the dark tracery of hedges across the sloping fields, and a line of elms holding their stiff shapes against the skyline. But once, thousands of years ago, when the landscape of the valley was rougher and simpler and they, unworn as yet by wind and rain, stood higher, they had perhaps been visible from far away, gaunt guardians of the valley, grey shapes against a grey sky.

The children knew the Stones well: ever since they could remember they had scrambled up their rough sides, jumped from one to another, and played hide and seek amongst them. The village people called them The Whispering Knights, and believed strange things of them – or at least, like the barn, told stories of them and then laughed as though they knew better than to believe. You must not move them, or ill fortune would follow you for ever. At night the fairies came from a hole in the hillside and danced around them, and at midnight the Stones themselves arose and danced in the air. They watched over the valley: in times of trouble they would leave their field and move. For centuries they had been undisturbed, the plough circling them every year to leave them standing, waist-deep in grass, in their ancient place. But recently a white fence had been built around them, and every few weeks in summer a man came to cut the grass. A neat green notice with white lettering said 'Ministry of Works. The Hampden Stones. A prehistoric stone circle for ritual purposes. Entrance free at all reasonable times.'

'That's a silly notice,' said Susie. 'I mean, they've got to say "Entrance free", haven't they? There's no one to give you a ticket, or take any money. It's just so you don't go thinking you're getting something for nothing.'

'And what would be an unreasonable time, anyway?' William added.

The notice always irritated them. They felt it to be intrusive: the Stones had always been a private place of theirs. But hardly anyone visited the Stones. The road was almost a mile away and although a green and white sign pointed across the fields few people ventured out onto the track along the hedgerows and up the hill. Most visitors would stop their cars at the roadside, stare vaguely out over the fields, and then drive on.

The children climbed up the hill, lapped by the rustling of ripe barley, leaving the noises of the road

and the village behind them, until they reached the Stones. Then, performing what had become an automatic ritual, they counted them.

'Twenty-nine,' said William, with satisfaction, and sat down on the grass.

There were always twenty-nine. That was another story about the Stones – that you could never count them and reach the same total twice, but the children had demonstrated time and again that this was not so. There were twenty-nine.

Martha climbed up on the tallest stone and stared out across the valley, the wind pulling her hair and flattening her clothes against her body. 'We should see the road again soon,' she said. 'The corn's the right colour.'

They had first seen it last summer. It was William's father who had told them that at Stonehenge, if you looked carefully from the right place, you could see the faint trace of an old, old road, straight as a die, leading from away over Salisbury Plain to the stone circle. 'It was for processions,' he explained. 'And I've always thought there might have been one leading to our Stones, but I've never been able to see it.'

The children had often stood at the edge of the circle, staring out over the valley in winter, summer, autumn and spring, but they'd never seen anything. Until one day last summer, when the corn was high and tawny, and then suddenly they'd seen it, a faint darker trace across the field, like a delicate line drawn with a paint-brush, reaching through the hedge and over the next field until it melted away into the distance. And then, when the corn was cut, it vanished, and, stare as they might, they never saw it on the rich dark plough of winter, or the sharp green of the spring corn.

William climbed up beside her and stared down into the valley, but the barley was moving in the wind, seething and rippling like the sea. 'It's better when the sun's out, anyway,' he said. 'It's too cloudy today.'

You could see a lot from the Stones. The valley lay spread out before you, all soft greens and yellows, with a glint of the river in the distance, and the rows of houses at the edge of Chipping Ledbury. And, much nearer, the grey of the road through the village, and the familiar spread of the village houses, gathered comfortably round the church.

'There's a funeral,' said Martha suddenly. 'Look at that great posh car going through the village.'

They looked. 'Nobody's died,' said Susie. 'I'd know, wouldn't I?'

'Well, it's stopped in the village,' said William, 'or we'd see it come out the other end.'

It went without saying that no one in Steeple Hampden owned an enormous, black car.

Susie pursed her lips, and frowned. 'It's time we were going back anyway,' she said. She began to walk quickly across the fields, followed by the others.

A short cut into the back of the village took them out along the lane next to the Poulters' shop.

'There it is,' said William.

It was an enormous black Rolls Royce, parked at one side of the road right opposite the shop, incongruously large against the cottages, so that the top of it reached almost to the upstairs windows. In the front seat sat a uniformed chauffeur, and behind, beyond a glass partition, two other people. Outside the shop stood Mrs Poulter and a few neighbours, talking and occasionally shooting surreptitious glances at the car and its occupants. Susie bustled up to her mother.

'Who is it, Mum?'

'It's that Mr Steel. Come to give us a look over, I suppose. See what he's up against, like. They've been sat there nearly five minutes, without so much as a "Good morning".'

Everybody stared at the car with hostility. 'That'll be his new wife with him,' said one of the women. 'Can't see her properly. They say she's ever so good-looking.'

'That's a nice bit of mink she's got on,' said Mrs Poulter knowingly. 'They don't grow on trees, coats like that.'

'Fancy wearing a fur coat in August,' said someone else.

'If I had a coat like that I'd wear it,' said Mrs Poulter with feeling.

Susie rejoined the others and passed on the information. They stood by the side of the road and looked at the car with interest.

'Those cars can do a hundred miles an hour,' said William. 'And they weigh several tons.'

'Beastly man,' said Susie venomously. 'I'd like to give him a piece of my mind, I would.'

There was a faint, powerful rumbling. The car engine had been started. Imperceptibly, it began to move down the road, towards the children. Mrs Poulter and her companions watched it go and then turned away with regret.

Susie, Martha and William stood in the shade of the churchyard wall, and very slowly, the car moved towards them, its great tyres whispering softly on the surface of the road. The chauffeur sat bolt upright, his gloved hands on the wheel, a peaked cap pulled forward on his forehead. The two people sitting far apart on the wide leather seat in the rear compartment were coming into view now. On the far side was an elderly man in a dark suit. He turned and glanced without interest at the children, looked up for a moment at the church, and then stared ahead, frowning slightly.

Beside him was a woman. Her hands, with bright rings on the fingers, were folded in her lap and her long legs crossed. Her head was turned away, and the children saw only straight, shining black hair lying sleekly against her skull. And then, as the car drew alongside them, she turned and looked straight at them.

It was a long face, pale, and the mouth was turned down at the corners as though it never smiled. Her skin was bone-white, and slightly gleaming, and the hair hung straight to her shoulders and shone like water. For long seconds she stared at them as the car slid by, and her eyes were terrible. They were black, and cold as frost, and quite empty of anything but a furious intent to destroy.

None of them moved a muscle. Afterwards, when the car had slipped silently away up the road, it seemed as though they stood there, like stones, for whole minutes, with the wall rough and warm against their backs and the rooks sliding in the air above their heads.

And then at last William spoke. 'We'd better go and see Miss Hepplewhite,' he said. 'We'd better tell her Morgan has actually been here, in Steeple Hampden.'

Five

Miss Hepplewhite took the news calmly. It was only to be expected, she said.

'She looked like an ordinary person at first,' said Martha. 'At least not ordinary really – she was very grand, in that car and everything. But when she looked at us it was quite different. Then you *knew*.' She shivered.

'Avoid looking at her,' said Miss Hepplewhite. 'She has certain hypnotic powers, if you are inclined to be suggestible.'

'What happens now?' asked William. 'We're not just going to sit about waiting to see what she does next, are we?'

'I think this campaign of your father's deserves some attention,' said Miss Hepplewhite. 'At least it will serve to annoy her, and perhaps sting her into making a false move.'

William's father was deeply involved in the war against the road. He was a mild man: William had never seen him so aroused before. Their home had become a kind of centre of operations, full of paper, lists of names, maps, ringing telephones and people coming and going. William and the girls were allotted a row of cottages behind the pub. They were to call at each cottage, show the occupants the map of the village as it was now, and the second one of how it would be when the road was built, and tell them how they personally would be affected. And then, if they objected to the scheme ('Which of course they will,' said William, 'unless they're barmy'), they could be invited to sign the petition.

'I'll start this end,' said William. 'I want to go on my own. You two can go together and we'll meet in the middle.'

There was only an old lady in the first cottage he called at. She was very deaf, and it took several minutes of hard shouting to get across to her what he had come about.

'I paid me rent day before yesterday,' she kept saying.

'It's not about the rent,' yelled William, trying to be

patient. I mean, honestly, he thought, boys don't come to collect the rent, do they?

'You never know what they'll try these days,' said the old lady, as though reading his thoughts, and he blushed guiltily. But at last, when he had spread the maps out on her dresser, they achieved an understanding. She signed her name with a flourish.

'There! Now they rogues'll not get my cottage, will they?'

'I hope not,' said William.

The next cottage was crawling with small children. The maps and the petition acquired several prints of sticky fingers and smears of jam before William could make his escape. Their mother was not at first entirely willing to sign.

'Might be the best thing for us, for all I know, mightn't it? We'd maybe get a bigger house. I'm sick to death of this old place. Suppose they gave us a council house?'

'Suppose they didn't?' said William quickly. 'I've heard there's difficulties.'

She looked at him with suspicion. 'What do you know about it, then?' He tried hard to look like someone with inside information, and was relieved when one of the children began screaming and she signed quickly to get rid of him, shrugging her shoulders.

In the next cottage there was old Mr Sampson, the school caretaker. 'Hello, there, son. Ah, you'll be come about your dad's petition. Come along in, then.'

William spread the maps out on Mr Sampson's kitchen table. Mr Sampson hooked his glasses on the end of his nose and pored over them, tutting and murmuring. 'Right through my vegetable garden, I reckon. Oh, it's a bad business, this, a bad business.'

William, looking out of the window, said suddenly, 'I didn't realize you could see the Hampden Stones from here. You can't from most places in the village.'

'Oh, aye. We're up a bit, see. The land rises a bit here. Well, we'll be needing them, you might say. It's time the Knights was coming back to look after their own, eh?' He darted a quick look at William over the top of his glasses.

'What?'

'You know the old story. They say as how the Stones were Knights in the old days, and they fought a great battle with a bad queen, and they won, and now they sits there to protect the valley, like.'

'Oh, yes,' said William vaguely, 'I know.' Through the open door he could see Susie stumping determinedly past with Martha trailing behind. He remembered that they were having a competition to see who could get the most signatures. 'Sorry, Mr Sampson, I must get on. You will sign it, won't you?'

'Oh, aye, I'll sign it all right. But I don't reckon as it'll do much good. We don't know what we're up against.'

William gave him a startled look.

'Those big men in London. You can't fight 'em.'

'Oh,' said William. 'Them. I see what you mean. Well, thanks very much. I must go now.'

They had collected a dozen signatures. 'Jolly good,' said William's father. 'We shall have almost a hundred per cent, by the time we're done. There's hardly anyone who won't sign it, and I'm getting people from miles around too, and from Chipping Ledbury. There's a lot of local feeling about it. Plenty of support for us.' He seemed full of optimism. 'They can't ignore public opinion. It would be quite scandalous. And I've got the editor of the *Gazette* on our side now,' he added

75

triumphantly. 'He's going to do a leader about it.'

Indeed, the newspaper article appeared the very next morning. William read it out to the others: 'The headlines says "Threat to Sharnbrook Valley". Then it goes on "This newspaper wishes to associate itself with the growing body of protest against the decision to re-route the M10 motorway through the Sharnbrook valley. It is difficult to understand how preference can have been given to this new route: under the previous scheme the motorway would have run south of Chipping Ledbury, through an area not distinguished for outstanding natural beauty or agricultural value, involving the demolition only of the Steel and Potter factory at Banton. Now, we understand that the road will run straight through the Sharnbrook valley, a famous Cotswold beauty-spot, and past the charming village of Steeple Hampden, where a number of cottages and farms will have to be obliterated to make way for it. The public has a right to know on what grounds this decision was taken, and why."'

'What's it mean?' asked Martha. 'It's got too many long words.'

'It just means they think we're right,' said William.

Susie scowled. 'Is the Chipping Ledbury *Gazette* important?' she asked.

William considered. He looked at the paper, which consisted largely of advertisements for cattle food and second-hand cars and innumerable photographs of wedded couples. He thought of the poky little office in Chipping Ledbury, between the coal-merchant and the butcher, with a lady in a grey cardigan typing at a desk and the shirt-sleeved editor visible beyond a glass partition.

'Well, not really, I suppose,' he said, with regret.

'Well then, it's not a lot of help, is it?'

'Still, it was very nice of them,' said Martha.

Susie sniffed. 'Being nice won't get rid of that road, will it?'

However, there were better things to come. Two days later the village appeared on a television news programme. It was strange to see the rich greens and golds of the valley translated into the grey world of the flickering screen.

'There's the church,' said William, 'and the pub. And there's the back of Mrs Hopkins going into her house. It all looks smaller, somehow.'

'There's Mum,' said Susie, peering into the grey depths, 'in the distance there, standing outside the shop. She put on her best coat special, when she saw the telly van and the cameras. I said no one would be able to see it properly, and you can't. You'd never know it's got a fur collar.'

The scene changed. In 'our Oxford studio' three men discussed the matter gravely from the depths of black leather chairs: an interviewer, the editor of the *Gazette*, and Mr Steel. Mr Steel was a balding man, fat, his face dissolving into a fleshy neck. His hands twitched on his lap as the camera closed in.

'Mr Steel,' said the interviewer, 'I understand that until just recently you were in favour of the decision to route the motorway through the site of your factory at Banton. Now you favour the Sharnbrook valley route. I wonder if you could tell us why?'

Mr Steel looked uncomfortable and reached frequently for the glass of water in front of him as he spoke. He said he had come round to the view that the demolition of the factory would not be in the best interests of the local community: he said that if the country wanted motorways then something had to go, didn't it? He spoke of taking the lesser of two evils, and how you couldn't make an omelette without breaking eggs. His eyes wandered frequently from the camera, and his speech was often dislocated, confused.

'You can tell he's been magicked,' said Susie, staring. 'It's obvious, isn't it?'

The editor of the *Gazette* became heated, and waved his arms about. He talked of 'behind-the-scenes activity' and 'unwarranted disregard of public opinion'. He had to be soothed by the interviewer and finally disposed of altogether as the scene faded out and the programme turned its attention to other matters.

'Our side won,' said William. 'Hands down. Anyone could see that. That Mr Steel was hopeless.'

The village was optimistic. Surely now that the world had seen the real nature of the problem, something would be done about it? They waited. For a day or two afterwards items appeared in national newspapers, headed 'Cotswold Valley Threatened', or 'Villagers Protest Against Motorway'. And then they realized they had faded completely from the public eye and everything was precisely as it had been before. William's father continued to write letters to newspapers, but only a few of them were printed. People became depressed and irritable as it slowly dawned on them that what had been an absorbing subject of conversation and a focus of interest, would before long become the unpleasant reality of a road through the valley, bringing with it mud, lorries, bulldozers, and the destruction of a place they loved.

'It's not going to do a blind bit of good, this petition,' said Mrs Poulter petulantly. 'I could have told them that. They'll build this road, come what may.'

'But Mum, you was all for it last week. You got the bread man to sign, and the Corona man, and Harris sausages and Birdseye, and Walls' ice-cream.'

'That'll do, Susie. You'll speak when you're spoken to, my girl.'

Affronted, Susie stamped off to find the others.

'My dad keeps getting in tempers about nothing, too,' said William. 'They can't help it really. You know something? I'm fed up with waiting. I wish something would happen.'

'Don't,' said Martha nervously, 'she might hear.'

'I don't care,' said William. They were passing the churchyard, on their way up to the barn, the chestnuts sighing above their heads. He threw his head back and shouted, 'I WISH SOMETHING WOULD HAPPEN. I'M NOT AFRAID OF YOU.' A cloud of rooks lifted from the trees, cawing indignantly.

'You'll have the vicar out,' said Susie. 'He gets hopping mad with people making a row in the churchyard.'

The day was sombre. Slaty clouds hung over the valley, so dark that a thread of smoke from a chimney looked white against them: their grey bellies seemed to brush against the line of elms on the top of the hill. Far away, beyond the river and the roofs of Chipping Ledbury, there was a paler rim of sky against the horizon. The children climbed over the gate and began to cross the field, ignored by the cows, grazing and swishing all round them. Presently they could see the front of the barn, the stone a soft grey today and the lichen on the rippling roof now a bright green.

'Hey!' said William. 'The doors are open.'

The girls looked. Sure enough, the big double doors of the barn gaped wide.

'Must've been us,' said Susie, 'last time we were up. Or else Miss Hepplewhite has been in there.'

'She doesn't usually.'

Martha suddenly clutched Susie's arm. 'There's someone there!'

Out of the darkness a figure materialized. It came to the entrance of the barn and stood there, looking out over the field. Far away as they were, they could pick out the white of her face, the gloss on her hair, and the fur coat slung over her back, the arms hanging emptily like an animal's pelt.

'Oh, William,' said Martha hysterically. 'I knew you shouldn't have said that!'

'Now you've gone and done it,' said Susie. 'What'll we do? Best run while we've got the chance, I reckon.'

But William did not hear them. As he saw Morgan in the entrance of the barn he felt the same slow, hot anger welling up inside him that he had felt when he first heard of the road. He was filled with the same outrage at this invasion of *his* place. He bristled: he choked; his face reddened. And then, all of a sudden, he broke away from the girls and began to run headlong over the grass, straight towards her, driven by rage, quite thoughtless of the consequences. His head pounded, his breath came in short gasps, and he felt enormous, rushing over the field in a fury. Morgan, by comparison, looked tiny, a remote, still figure in the black mouth of the barn.

The girls, on the other hand, saw a short figure in jeans and a battered sweater, stumbling over the molehills, arms and legs flailing, and Martha let out a moan of distress. She could not bring herself to look towards the barn again.

Susie yelled, 'Don't be daft! Come back.' But William was halfway across the field by now.

'Oh, Susie . . .' quavered Martha.

'Silly nit,' said Susie angrily. 'Now we're in a right mess. We can't just leave him, can we?' And she too began to run up the field. And Martha, because to be left standing there alone was even more appalling than to advance on the uncertainties ahead, followed her.

William was only yards from Morgan now. He did not look up, but kept running, feeling her stand there calm and silent somewhere in front of him, waiting. And then his fists shot out in front of him and he went into her with all his strength, hitting and butting.

Martha screamed. There was a wild hissing noise, like escaping steam, and William was flung back as though he had run into a wall, and rolled aside, clutching his head. And where Morgan had been standing there was a great column of smooth stone, as tall as a woman, rooted in the grass and looking out across the field. Far above, in the clouds, roofing the valley, there seemed to be a noise like a thin shriek, receding until the sky was silent again.

William dragged himself to his feet and staggered towards them. 'What happened?' he asked dizzily.

Susie pointed in silence. They all gathered round the stone, William rubbing his head.

'Don't,' said Martha. 'You're going to have a horrible bump on your forehead anyway. Are you all right?'

'I suppose so. It was jolly hard, I can tell you.' His knuckles too were red and bruised.

'What came over you?' asked Susie angrily. 'You don't know what might have happened. Have you gone daft or something, William?'

'It worked out all right, didn't it?'

'You were just lucky, that's what. Gave me a horrible fright, you did.'

'Don't go on, Susie,' said Martha. 'I was scared too, but it's all right now.'

She reached out gingerly and touched the stone. It was as smooth as an egg, and deeply veined like a pebble on a beach, a rich green in colour. It was tapered slightly at the top, giving it the merest suggestion of human form, and when Martha touched it it was as cold as ice, with a sharpness that stung her. She snatched her hand away.

'Leave it alone,' said Susie. 'Remember the cake!'

There was a footstep. Miss Hepplewhite had come through her gate and was walking quickly towards them.

'It was her!' cried William. 'Morgan! She was here! And now there's – this – instead!'

Miss Hepplewhite stood beside them and contemplated the stone. 'The green marble trick,' she said, 'that's an old favourite of hers.'

'Will she come back?' asked Martha, in a low voice.

'Oh, no.' Miss Hepplewhite tapped the stone unceremoniously with her stick and it sang, with a high, ringing note. 'No, she'll be far away by now. It was merely a means of escape.'

'Why did she bother?' asked Susie. 'It was only William. She's twice his size, and she's got these powers and all.'

William glared at her.

'Ah,' said Miss Hepplewhite, 'she dislikes physical contact and will avoid it whenever possible. Curiously, a direct attack is often the most effective, but few people have realized that. Astute of you, if I may say so,' she added, nodding at William with approval.

He flushed, and gave Susie a look. 'I didn't actually work it out or anything. I just got in a kind of fury when I saw her standing there. At our barn. I mean your barn.'

'The question is,' Miss Hepplewhite went on, reflectively, 'what do we do with it? It can't stay here. There'd be talk: we don't want people speculating about what they don't understand.'

'It's a nice stone,' said Martha. 'To look at, that is.'

'Precisely,' said Miss Hepplewhite. 'Just what I was thinking myself.' She stroked her chin thoughtfully. 'I've always fancied the idea of a piece of sculpture in the middle of my rose-garden. We'd need to work it a bit, of course. Perhaps we could make a hole through the middle of it – give it a more interesting shape. The problem is: how do we move it?'

'It's too heavy for a wheelbarrow,' said William, 'but I could get our car trailer. The three of us could pull it up your drive, and then through here and push the stone backwards into it.'

'It's got a nasty feel to it,' said Martha.

'We can wear gloves.'

'What a practical boy you are,' said Miss Hepplewhite. 'Onward into action, then. I shall be getting some refreshments ready.'

It took them some time to fetch the trailer. When at last, hot and tired, they had dragged it up to the barn, Martha was almost surprised to see the stone still there. The rain clouds had rolled away now, and the sky was high and turquoise above the valley. The stone looked somehow softer, and had lost its feeling of mysterious depth. And when Martha brushed against it inadvertently it was merely cool, with the ordinary chill of a lump of rock.

Miss Hepplewhite was waiting for them in the rose-garden with tall, frosted glasses of lemonade. After much debate she selected a site for the stone.

'Here, I think,' she said, 'among the floribundas. It will add height.'

After a great struggle they got it upright and into position. William had dug a shallow hole, but it still tended to rock a little. Miss Hepplewhite seemed unconcerned about that. She had produced, surprisingly, an electric drill, which she handed to William. 'I take it you are familiar with these things,' she said.

William took it, looking a little alarmed. 'I've used my dad's,' he said. 'What do you want me to do with it?'

There was a strange gleam in Miss Hepplewhite's eye. 'Right in the centre,' she said, 'about two feet down. A hole. We can enlarge it later with chisels.'

'I don't know if it'll go through marble,' said William dubiously. He advanced on the stone, and switched on the drill. There was an unpleasant whine. And then, as the drill touched the surface of the stone, at that precise moment, as they all watched, the whole thing melted, like the wax of a candle, and there was nothing left where it had been except a hole in the ground.

'Dear, dear,' said Miss Hepplewhite, 'all that effort for nothing.' She sounded oddly satisfied.

Martha looked at her and thought: I believe she knew all along that was going to happen. Miss Hepplewhite began casually snipping dead heads off the roses with a pair of secateurs: the expression on her face was quite inscrutable.

'We'd best be going home,' said Susie. She was still disgruntled. Both the others had proved equal to the challenge of Morgan, one way and another. She nearly

84

got me with that cake, she thought, and that's a fact: but William goes for her like she was another boy in the playground at school and she ups and turns herself into an old stone.

But William, secure in his triumph, could afford to be generous.

'Jolly good thing she saw you coming up behind,' he said carelessly, 'or I dunno what would have happened.'

Susie took a deep breath. 'Think that's what did it?'

'Sure, must've been.'

'Oh. Oh, I see.'

Six

In the night Martha dreamed. She dreamed of a sea: it was a milky-green sea, flecked with foam and veined with colour, like liquid marble. It seemed to be calling her, with soft, enticing voices, and when she sank into it it was warm and enfolding like a bed, but somewhere, far away, in another world, there was a thin voice screaming. She woke, slowly, and the enfolding warmth was her bed, and somewhere outside the window there was a strange noise. She was dizzy with sleep and most reluctant to wake up, but when she turned back under the blankets the noise was still there and she knew she could not ignore it. She rolled out of the bed and groped her way over to the window.

Outside it was unexpectedly bright: the garden, and her mother's washing on the line, and the fields beyond were all clear in a dark, colourless moonlight. The moon, a perfect circle, hung above the hill, and from time to time clouds slid across its face like hungry grey fish. She could see the fragile outlines of the elms, slightly darker than the sky, and the sloping fields on the hillside, striped with the black lines of the hedges. It was windy: the trees in the garden, and the tops of the hedges, quivered and stirred like seaweed in a current, and there were noises – of a dustbin lid rolling in the lane, and of the wind itself, banging and sucking at the walls of the houses. And somewhere high above it all, in the sky, or a long way away up on the hill, there was a high scream. It came, and it died away, and then sobbed again, and it might have been the wind, and it certainly was nothing human or animal.

Martha, standing there by the window, knew that she was hearing something people are not meant to hear, but at the same time she felt neither frightened nor curious. She was chill and numb, but something kept her on her feet and out of the warm bed. And then, as she looked across at the field on the hillside, a cloud swept clear of the moon and everything was suddenly very bright, and where the field had been a blank square moments ago it was broken now by a line of grey shapes. It was too far away to see if they were moving: they were spread out across the corn and they were the same size as human figures, but Martha knew they were not, and she did not need to count them. The wind was gusting now, sighing and moaning and clawing at the trees. The washing on the line flapped and cracked, and the moon was blotted out again by a pile of ragged cloud. And above it all, louder and nearer, came the scream, all around and above the house. Martha stood without moving, except that her eyes became very wide and round, the pupils opened like a cat's, and then she turned and walked stiffly to the bed, got in, and was asleep again within seconds.

Susie arrived to collect Martha after breakfast. Mrs Timms was washing up at the sink and the little boys were playing in the yard. Martha sat at the table eating cornflakes, her hair not brushed. 'Can Martha play?' asked Susie, popping a crust of toast into her mouth and absorbing the fact that the Timms' had had bacon for breakfast and Mrs Timms was wearing a new apron.

Mrs Timms, through steam and gushing taps, said that Martha seemed a bit off colour today and perhaps she was sickening for something. Susie gave Martha a critical glance and said, 'There wasn't anything wrong with her yesterday.'

'Do you feel all right, dear?' asked Mrs Timms. 'You haven't said a word this morning.'

'I'm all right,' said Martha, sounding sullen. Mrs Timms looked at her for a moment, and turned back to the sink.

'It's the weather,' said Susie chattily. 'It was a shocking night. Mum said she was up and down till all hours shutting windows and that. It kept me awake.'

'Is that it, Martha?' said Mrs Timms. 'Did you hear the gale?' But Martha shook her head, and went on eating cornflakes in silence. She seemed not to be paying much attention to them.

'Well, come on then,' said Susie. 'We're going down to the river. William's got his fishing-rod – he's outside the shop.'

Martha got up obediently and moved towards the door. The two small boys had come in a moment before and when Susie had finished speaking they set up a clamour of, 'Can we come too? Can't we fish too?' Martha stared at them without any expression, and Mrs Timms, from the sink, shook her head and said something half inaudible about them being too young and it not being safe down there.

Tommy, the younger, began to wail. Susie looked at him and felt suddenly generous and capable. 'I'll look after them, Mrs Timms. I'm used to looking after my little brother,' she said. 'We're only going to the bathing-place by the bridge. It's ever so shallow and I won't let them go in the water anyway.' Martha said nothing: she still looked oddly blank, almost dazed.

Mrs Timms shut the taps off and turned round. 'Well, if you don't mind, dear. You're sure you'll watch them carefully? Don't let them lean over the bridge.'

Susie promised, and the four of them set off to join William.

He was waiting outside the shop, fiddling with the reel on his fishing-rod. He looked with dismay at the small boys. 'Gosh, Martha, what've you brought the little 'uns for? We'll be spending all the time minding they don't fall in the river.'

Martha looked at him blankly, and Susie said, 'She didn't. I said I'd look after them. Wake up, Martha, are you still asleep or something?'

They set off for the river, Susie marshalling the small boys on each side of her and Martha trudging a few yards behind.

'It was good yesterday,' said William cheerfully, 'the business with the stone. We beat her again, didn't we?'

'I s'pose so,' said Susie. 'We do, when it's things like dragons and stones. When it's the bigger things she wins, doesn't she? I don't know – I feel creepy today. Like something wasn't quite right.'

'What do you mean? You sound like Martha. It's she has feelings about things, not you. Isn't it?' William turned to look back at Martha, who did not reply.

'What's up with her? She in a mood or something?'

'I don't know. She's been funny since I went to fetch her. P'raps she's poorly.'

They both turned to look curiously at Martha, who was trailing along, staring at the ground.

'Oh, well,' said William, 'she'll probably be all right soon. Cheer up, Martha.'

They were making for the bathing-place. This was a point on the Sharnbrook about half a mile beyond the village, over the fields, where the narrow stream widened out into a shallow gravelly place, fringed with reeds and stooping willows. The water, nibbling at the soft muddy bank, had eaten away a great, still pool for itself before it swept away again round a corner and wound off through the fields, and here, on a good day, you could catch minnows, or even a stripy perch. At one end of the pool there was a humped stone bridge, leading now from nowhere to nowhere, but once there must have been a road across the fields here, for the bridge was wide enough for carts and wagons. Teazles grew high on the banks; a moorhen guided her squadron of chicks in and out of the reeds; and from time to time a water-rat plopped out of a hole in the bank and chugged away downstream, half-submerged.

Susie arranged the boys on the crescent of gravelled beach at the foot of the bridge and sat down to keep an eye on them. William wandered off to select a good fishing-place and Martha stood on the bridge, staring glumly into the water. There were noises of birds and insects, and above everything else the busy rushing of the river under the bridge, where it narrowed between the stone piers and swept through, with green weed streaming just under the surface. William tried fishing there, but found the water too fast, and moved away. He tried the beach, but it was too shallow and anyway the small boys had disturbed the fish, so he crossed back over the bridge and plunged into the tangle of willow-herb and teazles that crowned the bank. Here, at the point where the stream began to narrow again before the corner, he found a place where he could push through and lie on his stomach, overlooking the water. He was screened from the others by a rise in the bank further along, but he could hear distantly the cries of the boys and Susie ordering them about. He settled down to fish.

After a quarter of an hour he had caught nothing, and then, maddeningly, the hook caught in a mass of weed under the bank. He tried to ease it out, then got irritated and tugged. The line snapped, and came up without the hook. He had another one, and more line, so he set to repairing it. But the line was fine nylon, slippery and almost impossible to tie. He dropped one of his spare hooks and lost it in the undergrowth: finally, infuriated, he put down the line and went to fetch Susie. It was the sort of thing she would be able to do much better than he, and without losing another precious hook.

'Why didn't you bring the rod here?' said Susie. 'I shouldn't leave the little 'uns.'

'I didn't think. Come on, it won't take a minute.'

The boys were admonished not to leave the beach. Martha was standing a few yards away still, by the bridge. 'Don't let them go in the water,' instructed Susie, and Martha nodded vaguely, without looking up. Susie and William scrambled away up the bank and vanished round the corner among the teazles.

Martha stood looking at the water, but not really seeing anything. She felt sleepy, and very heavy and lethargic, and she didn't care about anything at all. She had followed the others down to the river, but she wasn't really interested in whether she was with them, or at home, or somewhere quite different. She had a vague impression of not having slept well the night before, but she could not remember being awake. A fish splashed in the pool, and she watched it without interest.

There was a step on the bridge, and she looked up. A short, stocky woman was standing just above her, looking down. She must have come across the field quite

noiselessly. She wore a baggy tweed skirt and jersey, ankle socks and heavy shoes, and a haversack over one shoulder. There was a scarf tied around her head and her face was almost completely swamped by very large dark glasses. Martha looked away again: one often saw people like that wandering around the village and the valley during the summer.

'Good morning,' said the woman.

'Good morning,' said Martha dully, kicking a stone into the water.

'What a delightful place,' said the woman, in a deep, soft voice. 'I think I must have lost my way coming out of the village.'

Martha tried to drag up the energy to reply. 'Were you looking for the Hampden Stones?' she said at last. 'That's what people come here to look at. They're the other way – through the village and up the hill.'

The woman drew in her breath with a little hissing noise. 'Oh, no, dear. I wouldn't want to go up there, would I? That's a bad place, isn't it, dear? We mustn't go there.'

Martha looked at her, frowning stupidly. The sun kept catching the woman's glasses and flashing, making Martha blink and squint. She opened her mouth to disagree, and unaccountably found herself saying something quite different.

'That's right,' she said meekly. 'It's a bad place. We mustn't go there.'

The small boys had stopped playing and were squatting on the gravel, watching warily. Tommy said, 'Martha, come here, come over here.' Martha twitched her shoulders irritably and ignored him. She was still looking at the woman.

The woman took a step forward. 'We'd better be going, dear,' she said. 'You're coming with me, aren't you, Martha?'

'That's right,' said Martha, quite passive. 'I'm coming with you.'

The woman held out her hand and Martha took it. They began to walk away over the bridge. The boys stood up, staring after them. Tommy shouted, 'Martha! Martha, come back! Don't go away!' But Martha took no notice. She didn't even turn round. For a little while her head, beside that of the woman, could

93

be seen above the corn as they followed the path to the road, and then it vanished.

Susie and William slithered down the bank and came back onto the beach. The line had broken several times, and they had already lost the only surviving hook. William had decided he must find a less weedy place to fish in.

'Where's Martha?' asked Susie, looking round.

'She went with the lady,' said Tommy, pointing up the path.

Susie stared, and William put down the fishing-rod. 'What lady?'

'The lady that came just then.'

Susie and William looked at each other. 'Was it a lady you knew?' said Susie very sharply, grabbing Tommy by the shoulder.

Tommy wriggled away indignantly. He shook his head. 'I never seen her.'

Susie squatted down in front of him and said urgently, 'Was it a tall lady with black hair, Tommy? And a sort of white face. With a fur coat on?'

Tommy shook his head again. 'She were one of those ladies with sack things on their backs and big boots for walking. She had big black specs on.'

Susie and William looked at each other, this time with relief. Susie said, a bit sheepishly, 'Just for a moment I thought . . .'

'So did I,' said William.

'All the same,' said Susie, 'she oughtn't to go off with strangers like that. We've been told.'

'We'd better go after her. P'raps she was just showing her where the road is.'

They began to hurry along the path, with the barley crackling beside them and the swallows looping and swerving a few yards above their heads. For some reason, they found themselves hurrying more and more, until they were running over the summer-dried ruts, with the younger ones panting behind. There was no sign of Martha, and the track lay straight in front of them all the way to the road. Cars slid past every few minutes, their tops just visible above the hedge.

They covered the last twenty yards or so as though it were a race, and jumped the stile into the road. Further down the road, away from the village, a big oak tree grew out of the hedge, throwing a pool of shadow on the roadside. The Rolls was standing in the shadow, and Martha and the woman were just getting into it. Martha was holding the woman's hand, very docile, and she did not look round at Susie's scream, but the woman turned and stared back at them before she climbed into the back of the car. It started up at once and slid quickly out of sight.

All the way back to the village Susie could not stop talking. 'Trust Martha to do a thing like that! That's Martha all over, isn't it? What'll we do, William? We got to go after her, haven't we? I mean, it stands to reason, doesn't it? Oh, I'll have something to say to you, Martha Timms! Right dope she is . . .'

'It's all right, Susie,' said William. 'It'll be all right, honestly. We'll do something, don't worry.'

'It's my fault. I could see she was all funny today. I thought she was poorly.'

'It'll be all right,' said William again. 'Please don't go on.'

They bundled the small boys unceremoniously through the back door of their cottage, with instructions to say that Martha was still with the others and would be back later.

'I can't tell Mrs Timms,' said Susie. 'I just can't. She'd go mad. We've got to do something ourselves. There's only us.'

They went straight to find Miss Hepplewhite. She was making jam in her kitchen. There was a thick smell of fruit and sugar, and drunken wasps crawled on the windows. When they told her what had happened she sat down, and they saw that her hands on the arms of the chair were trembling.

'Why did she *go* with her like that?' said Susie in anguish. 'I mean, Martha's a bit dreamy, but she's not daft.'

'Never mind that now. Morgan has her ways. You say she seemed strange today? Martha, I mean?'

The children nodded. 'Kind of half-asleep,' said Susie.

Miss Hepplewhite drummed her fingers on the table, deep in thought.

'Look,' said William, 'if Morgan can just change herself like that, how are we ever going to know who she is?'

'She is quite recognizable when you are on your guard,' said Miss Hepplewhite. 'The eyes give her away, normally. But some people are always more vulnerable to her than others. Now the thing is – we must get Martha back before the poor child becomes her creature. There is no time to be lost. This time we have to carry the war into her camp. Are you prepared to do that?'

'You bet,' said William. 'Poor old Martha . . . But where could Morgan have taken her?'

'Wherever her stronghold is at the moment.'

They looked at each other in perplexity. Then Susie said suddenly, 'I know. Mr Steel's got that great big house just outside Chipping Ledbury. Clipsham Manor. I went there once – they open the gardens to the public at Easter for two bob each. D'you think she's there?'

'Very likely,' said Miss Hepplewhite reflectively. 'Very likely. Large. Private. Yes, I think that is where you will find Martha . . .'

They waited by the roadside a few hundred yards out of the village. There was no bus for another hour and a half, so the only thing was to hitch-hike. For ten minutes or so cars flashed past with no sign of stopping, and then at last a lorry pulled up beside them with a hiss of brakes. The driver leaned out of his cab, high above them. 'Bit young for this game, aren't you? Your mums know what you're up to?'

William went scarlet, but Susie stuck her thumbs into the pockets of her jeans and said haughtily, 'We got to get to Chipping Ledbury. Will you take us?'

The lorry-driver tipped a cigarette out of a packet, stuck it in the corner of his mouth and looked at them speculatively. 'All right then, hop in.'

They pulled themselves up the high step and sat on one end of the bench seat, crowded together against the door. The man drove fast, staring ahead and whistling softly through his teeth. Once he pushed a bag of sweets towards them along the seat but Susie shook her head and said nothing, her lips pulled together in an obstinate line.

'You want to watch it, you know,' said the man. 'You don't want to go picking up lifts like that. There's some odd folk around. You never can tell.'

'I know,' said Susie, very cool.

The man looked sideways at her. 'How old are you?'

Susie didn't answer.

'All right, suit yourself, love. Where'll I put you down?'

'Just outside Chipping Ledbury'll do,' said Susie, 'if you're going through.'

'And thank you,' added William.

The man laughed suddenly. 'That's all right, son.'

They rattled into the town, and wasted precious minutes waiting at traffic lights and sitting, throbbing, in an endless traffic jam in the High Street. The children sat forward on the edge of the seat, stiff and tense.

'Oh, come on,' said William under his breath.

The driver looked at them curiously. 'What's the hurry, then?'

'We're meeting someone,' said Susie.

At last they were through the town and out the other side. A high wall loomed ahead on the right, and wrought-iron gates.

'Here,' said Susie suddenly. 'Can we get out here?'

The lorry screeched to a halt at the roadside. The driver looked round and observed that there didn't seem much to get out for.

'It'll do fine,' said William hastily. 'Thanks very much.' They slid out of the door and jumped to the grass verge. The driver shrugged, grinned, and drove off. They were alone on the empty road, with the high iron gates and long driveway to Clipsham Manor on the other side of the road.

They crossed over, and walked through the open gates. The gravelled drive, with tall chestnuts at either side, swept through parkland. In the distance the chimneys and roof of an enormous house could just be seen above the screen of a high hedge. The children began to walk up the drive, not on it, where they would be conspicuous, but to one side, on the grass under the trees.

They were watching and listening as they walked, darting suspicious glances out across the park and back over their shoulders, and listening for the sound of a voice or footstep above the rustling of the leaves and the croak of rooks overhead.

At the end of the drive was a high, dense yew hedge. The drive swept away to the right in the direction of stables and outbuildings, but there was a gap in the hedge wide enough to admit cars. A notice to one side of it said 'Goods and Trade Vehicles to the Rear Entrance Only'. They sidled through the gap, keeping close in the shadow of the hedge, and the front of the house came into full view, with a gravelled circle in front of it.

It was very large. Rows of windows stretched away to either side of a great sweep of steps leading up to the front door. Tubs of blue hydrangeas flanked the steps and at the bottom twin stone lions on pillars squinted out over the countryside. It was quiet: there was no sign of life at all except for the distant sound of a lawn-mower.

The windows glittered blackly in the sunshine: they might or might not conceal watching eyes.

Dead centre of the gravelled circle the Rolls was parked, glistening like a well-fed seal.

Seven

They crouched behind the hedge, watching.

'She's there all right,' said Susie. 'Must be. Now what'll we do?' Gloom descended on her: the house was vast, impregnable, and they had no business there. Not only was there the fear of Morgan, but also the more ordinary fear of people who might appear and demand what they thought they were doing.

'What'll we do?' she said again. She felt very much in need of reassurance.

William's face was all screwed up, as though in pain – a sure sign of thought with him. He had a smear of black oil down one cheek, presumably acquired during the lorry-ride. 'They'll have hidden her somewhere. We'll just have to look, won't we? You're not scared, are you?'

'Oh, no,' said Susie hastily. She pulled her plait round and began to chew hard.

'I know,' said William, 's'pose we try to find whoever was driving the car? There was a bloke in a peaked cap and a uniform the first time we saw it, wasn't there?'

'A chauffeur. That's what they're called.'

'A what? Well, him, anyway. I mean, he'll know if she brought Martha here, won't he? And he might tell us where she is.'

'Unless he's on Morgan's side.'

'Well, we've got to try something, haven't we? Come on.'

Susie remembered, from her visit at Easter, that there were stables and garages round at the back of the house. They retreated to the drive, keeping close up to the hedge all the time, and began to follow it round.

It ended at an archway leading into a cobbled yard. The yard was walled at one end, and the other three sides were stables and garages, with rooms above. White pigeons walked on the roof, picking at the lichen and rumbling contentedly. There were signs of activity: from an open window came the clatter of dishes and the sound of a wireless playing quietly, and as they peered cautiously through the archway a man came out of a garage, carrying a bucket, and walked briskly across to a car parked on the cobbles. He set the bucket down with a clatter, fished a cloth out of it and began to wash the car, humming to himself.

'That's him,' whispered Susie. 'Least I think it is.'

William looked round the yard. There was a chair set against the wall at one end, with a uniform slung over the back of it and a peaked cap on the seat. He looked back at the man cleaning the car.

'Go on,' hissed Susie. 'You go and ask him. I did the bit with the lorry-driver.'

William hesitated. He wiped his hands on the sides of his jeans: they felt oddly clammy. And his heart was bumping about in his chest in the most peculiar way. The man looked a perfectly ordinary man, but you never knew . . . He glanced sideways at Susie: she looked quite calm, biting away at her plait.

'Go on,' she said again. 'What's up?'

William took a deep breath, and walked boldly out into the yard.

The man looked up. 'Yes?' he said curtly, with a quick glance at William's grubby jeans and shirt. 'The place isn't open today, you know. Easter and Bank Holidays only.'

'It's not that,' said William awkwardly. 'I wanted to ask you something.'

'You'd better be quick,' said the man. 'They don't like people hanging around. Not unless you've got business here.' He glanced towards the archway. 'What do you want?'

'It's about the car,' said William, 'the big one. The Rolls. The girl that got into it this morning – she's a friend of ours. There's been some sort of mistake – she didn't really mean to come here. We've got to take her home. Please – do you know where she is?'

The man leaned on the car and stared at William. 'I don't know what you're at,' he said. 'There isn't any girl here, far as I know. The Rolls hasn't been out today.'

William felt himself go hot and cold. 'Yes,' he said desperately. 'Yes. Honestly. We saw it. In Steeple Hampden. Perhaps she – the lady – Mrs Steel, I mean – p'raps she was driving it.'

'She can't drive,' said the man. 'I drive the Rolls. Always. And I'm telling you it hasn't been out today. You've got mixed up with some other car. And now clear off, son. You'll get me into trouble if they take it into their heads to come round here, and see you.'

William moved backwards, his heart thumping. 'I'm sorry,' he said. 'Sorry. I'll go now. I'm sorry I bothered you.'

'It's okay. Just that she's got a nasty temper, see, and I've got my orders about seeing strangers off the place.'

'Sorry,' said William again. He turned to go. The desperation in his voice made the man call after him.

'Here, just a minute. If there's really some girl gone off in a car you ought to tell the police, you know.'

'It's all right,' said William. 'It doesn't matter. It's nothing. Really.'

'All right, then, son. And now beat it, there's a good boy.'

William rejoined Susie. They conferred in whispers behind the wall, frantic.

'*I know* it was the same car. D'you think he's – like Morgan?'

'No,' said William. 'He wasn't telling lies. I could tell that. He was an ordinary person. I don't understand about the car, though.'

The sun had gone in. There was a cool wind licking at their bare arms: rings of dust swirled on the drive.

'You know,' said Susie suddenly, 'I don't like it here. It's a horrible place. I'm scared, and that's a fact.'

'Oh,' said William, relieved, 'are you? Matter of fact, so am I.'

'Everything looks ordinary, but you feel it isn't really.'

'That's right. Martha'd say it was creepy.'

Susie nodded. They looked at each other. 'But we've got to go on. Stands to reason, doesn't it?'

'We'll have to go into the house,' said William, 'and look for her. It's the only thing.'

They walked away, keeping very close to each other.

They decided to approach the house from the back: to venture across that sweep in the front, and up those great steps, would leave them as exposed as flies on a wall. At least round the back the gardens would give them cover. They found a path that led from the stables through a walled kitchen garden and then out behind the house. A wide terrace stretched the length of the building, with long windows opening onto it. Below was a neat rose-garden, the beds edged with a low box hedges, and beyond that a great stretch of lawn, dotted with sweeping cedars. Far away at one end of it a man with a lawn-mower crawled up and down, banding the grass with paler stripes. Beyond the lawn the park rolled away into the distance: black and white cows grazed and someone on a white horse cantered lazily among clumps of oak and birch.

The children kept close to the house. They found themselves under an open window, and from inside came noises of a tap running, somone beating with a wooden spoon, and women's voices talking. The kitchens.

'You want to be careful with that mayonnaise,' said a voice. 'There'll be ructions if it's too oily. She likes it thin.'

Another woman's voice said something they could not hear.

'And she's got a really 'orrible temper. I wouldn't like to get across her, I wouldn't. She's got a way of looking that gives you the creeps.'

'Sssh!' said the first voice.

'It's all right. I heard her go out horse-riding, and Mr Steel's at the office.'

More clattering. Noise of a kettle being filled. The first voice said: 'We'll have a cuppa, shall we? There's time.' Chairs scraped on a stone floor. 'Mind, she's got him where she wants him. You can tell who wears the trousers here. Things have changed, I can tell you, since she came – it seems a lot more than three weeks. Ever so easy going it was before.' The woman sighed.

'Come on,' whispered William, 'they're going to sit there for a bit. Let's go in.'

They crept up the flight of steps that led onto the

terrace, and paused outside the open windows of the first room. A curtain lifted a little in the breeze, but there was no sound from inside. They peered round the curtain, and went in.

It was a large room, the polished floor strewn with rugs. Stiff, unwelcoming chairs stood around the floor and the walls were plastered with dark oil paintings. They edged their way through it, trembling, their Plimsolls squeaking on the floor. William took his off and stuffed them into his shirt, and after a moment Susie did the same.

William opened the door and they found themselves looking into a round entrance hall. It was floored with black and white squares of stone, and light came from a dome high above their heads. The two arms of a staircase swept upwards from each side of them and immediately opposite were high, carved doors: one was half open, and showed the downward spread of the stone steps they had seen from outside, the parked Rolls, and beyond it the hedge behind which they had stood ten minutes ago. The hall was empty: there was not a sound.

They looked at each other. 'Up?' whispered William, and Susie nodded.

They crept up the staircase, the stone icy under their bare feet, feeling hideously exposed. If one of the doors opened now . . . But nothing happened. They found themselves on a long landing, confronted by a row of doors, all closed.

William took a deep breath, and opened the first one. Inside there was darkness, and a smell of furniture polish.

'Broom cupboard. It's your turn.'

Susie turned the next handle and pushed the door

open. There was an expanse of shining tiles. 'Bathroom. I say, the bath's black!'

'Never mind that. We haven't got time.' William opened the next door. It was a man's bedroom: there was a dressing-table with silver-backed brushes, and tweed jackets hanging against a cupboard. He closed it again.

'What are we looking for?'

'Martha. Or something to show she's been here.'

They opened two more doors and found two more bedrooms, neat and empty. Growing braver, they opened and closed cupboards, looked under beds. Nothing.

Before the last door William hesitated: somewhere underneath them a vacuum cleaner was rumbling.

'Come on,' said Susie. 'Hurry.'

He opened the door, and they found themselves looking into another, larger bedroom. Open windows looked out over the garden, and through them came the sound of a horse's hooves scraping on gravel. They ventured into the room across thick carpet: there were bottles on the dressing-table, and a woman's dress hung over a chair. A great shiver ran up Susie's spine and she began to rub her arms. She looked at William, and he said in a whisper, 'Yes, I can feel her too.'

With a deep chill gripping them they stood looking round, and then all of a sudden Susie saw it, lying screwed up on the carpet against the wall in one corner of the room. A toffee paper, red and white, such as her mother sold in the shop at ninepence a quarter.

At one side of the room there was a door. They ran to it and groped for the handle both at once. William burst it open, and they were looking into another, much smaller room.

Martha was sitting on a stool in the middle of the room, staring blankly at an empty fireplace. There was a half-full packet of toffees beside her, and some

picture-books, rather too young for her age, on a table nearby.

William stopped dead. 'Oh, Martha, we were so scared! Gosh – I'm glad we've found you! Are you all right?'

Susie felt a great flood of relief. She looked Martha up and down, from her unbrushed hair, down her crumpled cotton dress, to her grubby socks and shoes. Then she said in a disgruntled voice, 'We've been

looking all over for you. You are a daft thing, Martha
– the door's not locked. You could have walked out.'

Martha looked at them with polite interest, and said
nothing.

'Martha!' said William. 'What's up? Don't you
know who we are?'

'Yes,' said Martha flatly. 'You're William and she's
Susie Poulter.'

Susie took her firmly by the arm. 'Martha – come on!
She'll be back any minute.'

'That's right,' said Martha, without emotion, 'she'll
be back soon.'

'Help me, William,' said Susie, infuriated. 'We'll
have to get her out somehow.'

They heaved Martha to her feet and dragged her
between them back into the bedroom. She neither
cooperated nor resisted. They had almost reached the
door when they heard a sound from outside: the tap of
shoes on stone. Someone was coming up the stairs.
William hesitated, but Susie went on dragging Martha.

'We can't go back – there's no other way out. We've
got to get down the stairs.'

They opened the door and ran out onto the landing,
with Martha between them.

Morgan was on the staircase. She was wearing white
riding-breeches, a black jacket and high shiny boots.
Her face was a white mask, the eyes sunken and glow-
ing. For a moment William hesitated. He remembered
the last time: Miss Hepplewhite's words came back to
him – 'Direct attack is often the best thing.' And then
he felt her terrible eyes and a great dark fear swept
over him.

The children shot down the other side of the stairs,
slithering on the stone, pulling Martha between them.

They were so quick that they had reached the bottom before Morgan had time to turn and start to come down after them. As they ran through the open door and down the steps into the bright air they could hear her shouting something, but they did not hear what it was she said.

Across the gravel and through the hedge, and then they stopped, panting. It was very quiet, except for the gentle swishing of the chestnut trees and an aeroplane crawling somewhere high above their heads. The sky was ridged with grey cloud and a light, misty rain brushed their faces.

Susie said, 'Not along the drive – she could come after us with the car.'

They began to run over the grass through the parkland, dodging from one clump of trees to another, trying to avoid the open ground. In the distance they could see rooftops and curls of smoke, and they could hear the rumble of traffic on the road: the outskirts of Chipping Ledbury were a bare half-mile away.

For five minutes they ran without speaking, the ground hard and springy under their feet. Then they stopped for breath. William turned to look behind them.

'Don't!' said Susie. 'Better not to. Let's just get on as quick as we can. We'll be all right in Chipping Ledbury, where there's people everywhere.'

There was a distant drumming sound, and the ground seemed to tremble slightly: it must be the traffic, she thought.

They ran on, with Susie clutching Martha's hand all the time. She hadn't said a word since they had found her in that room, and her eyes still had that funny, fixed look. The drumming was getting louder: it seemed to fill the air around them and suddenly Susie could bear it no longer. She looked over her shoulder.

There was a white horse coming from the direction of the house, tearing over the grass at full gallop. Its mane and tail streamed out against the green, and although it was still some way away they could see the ripple of powerful muscles, and the flare of a nostril. The ground throbbed with the sound of its hooves, and on its back sat a dark figure, still and upright.

There was still two hundred yards between them and the line of trees that screened the park from the road, and all the while they were covering it the drumming of the hooves grew closer and closer, a dreadful, rhythmic beat, and they could hear the grunt of the horse's breathing and the chink of a stirrup, but they did not turn round. As they drew themselves into the trees it was a few paces behind them and they could hear its furious snorting as they scrambled over the iron railings and dropped down onto the roadside. Only Martha hung back, staring behind her with wide eyes, as though something were holding her, and Susie had to use all her strength to get her over and onto the road.

A few yards away a bus was just pulling up at the stop. They tore after it, and climbed onto the platform as the conductor was ringing the bell.

Gasping for breath, they piled into a seat. William found a shilling in his jeans' pocket and paid the fares. The conductor said amiably, 'Nearly had to wait for the next, didn't you?' and William nodded, speechless and white-faced.

'Where'll we go?' asked Susie.

'Home, I s'pose. But this one only goes to Chipping. We'll have to go to the bus station and wait for the one that goes to the village.'

Neither of them had any idea what time it was: it could have been morning, afternoon or evening. Fishing in the Sharnbrook could have been days ago, not an hour or two.

Susie turned to look at Martha. 'You feeling all right?'

Martha smiled tranquilly and said nothing. The others looked at her in doubt.

William whispered, 'She has been magicked, hasn't she?'

'I reckon so.'

'What'll we do with her?'

'Best leave her alone for a bit. Maybe it'll wear off now she's not with Morgan any more.'

The bus had reached the town. They got off at the stop in the High Street and began to walk along in the direction of the small bus station where they knew they would, eventually, be able to catch a bus home. The pavement was crowded with people, mostly women with shopping-baskets and babies in prams. Nobody gave them a second glance: they were three children, apparently in a hurry, one being pulled along by the other two. The shops were bright, exposed behind huge windows – garish tins arranged in vast columns and pyramids, cereal packets piled into shelving cliffs, and people moving silently among them like fish in a tank. William was struck by the thought that it would be impossible, quite impossible, to stop anyone here and explain what was happening to them. It was as though they, and Morgan, locked in their deadly game of hide-and-seek, were removed into a different layer of time. They could see people, and speak to them, but no longer communicate. And all the time the sky was growing darker, with rough, shifting clouds racing behind the rooftops and the pavement slippery with the misting rain.

They were halfway along the High Street now, with the bus station still some way to go. It was impossible to move very fast: they kept being washed to one side of the pavement by the crowds, and once or twice they were separated. William found himself walking alone and turned round to look for the girls: as he did so something on the other side of the road caught his eye.

The Rolls was parked against the pavement, empty.

Susie must have seen it at the same moment. She was hovering in the doorway of a greengrocer's, looking frantically round, holding Martha by the arm. William ran back to join her.

After a minute or so they saw Morgan. She was wearing a coat, with the collar turned up, and dark glasses, but there was no mistaking the gleam of her white skin, and the black hair capping her head. She was standing on the opposite side of the road, turning her head this way and that enquiringly, her glasses reflecting the movement of the street. One or two women glanced at her with curiosity, and passed by.

Martha saw her, and made a little sound. She took a step forward, and as she did so Morgan looked directly across at them, and began to move.

'Quick!' said Susie, and they hurried away, bumping into people, pulling Martha between them.

'Into a shop?' said William.

'No. Keep outside.'

There was something terrible about the thought of being shut in somewhere with Morgan. At least outside the sky was above you. They hurried on: but when Susie turned once to look behind them she caught a glimpse of Morgan in a gap between the shoppers, not far behind.

They were leaving the shops behind now, and the people on the pavement thinned out as the street widened into a green, with houses overlooking it at each side, and the church at the far end. There were children playing on the grass, and cars parked alongside the road which circled the green. Avoiding the open space, they kept close to the cars, dodging from one to another, looking nervously over their shoulders. Presently they saw Morgan, on the opposite side of the green. She was half-hidden from them by the cars, but they could just see her head above them, moving from side to side like a snake, searching, and as they moved on, so did she. In due course they would meet at the top of the green.

'This is a bad place,' said William. 'We're going to get trapped if we go on.'

They looked round. The houses presented a blank wall along each side of the green: there were no side roads, only the occasional alley ending in a row of dustbins and a blank wall.

Suddenly Susie said, 'The church! Miss Hepplewhite once said she hates churches. And churches always have a back door.'

They hurried on, ducking their heads below the cars, scurrying past the gaps. Their faces were wet with the spitting rain: the children playing on the green were leaving, drifting away into houses and down the street. They reached the church. William turned the big iron handle on the door and they stepped into a dusky coolness, smelling of stone and flowers.

Eight

The church was empty. At first they had been uncertain: you never could tell with churches. You could think yourself alone and then suddenly someone would slide from behind a pillar, arranging hymn books or flicking a duster, or a hidden organ would mysteriously come to life. But St Michael's, Chipping Ledbury, was, at this precise moment, empty except for the three children moving uneasily down the side aisle, to get further away from the door, and a bluebottle fizzing irritably somewhere high up against a dusty window. The children were dismayed. Susie hesitated.

'It doesn't make any difference,' said William. 'I mean, we're on our own anyway, aren't we? It's just us and her, isn't it?'

Susie nodded, glancing back all the time at the door through which they had come.

They reached the end of the aisle and found themselves looking through wrought-iron gates into a small chapel. Roses in glass jars were dropping their petals on a white altar-cloth and a stone knight and his lady lay stiffly on their tomb.

Susie said, 'There'll be a little room somewhere where the vicar puts his surplice on and that, like in our church, and it'll probably have a door to outside. Come on.'

They began to cross the church, under the altar rail and past the pulpit. The carpet was rolled back where someone had been rubbing a brass, and a long, helmeted face stared up at them from the floor. There

114

was a sickly smell from some lilies in a vase under the pulpit.

All of a sudden the door creaked. The children ducked down into a pew and crouched there, hardly breathing. They heard the door slowly open, and close again, and then there was silence, a silence that hung in the air like a thread, as though the slightest movement would break it. They kept quite still, though the cold was striking up at them from the stone floor and Susie could feel her teeth beginning to chatter.

At last William inched his head up to peer over the top of the pew. Morgan was standing by the door, with her back almost up against it, as though she did not want to leave it. There was something in her stance of horror and revulsion, like a cat that ventures into water, and her snake-eyes darted here and there, hunting the dark corners of the building.

William ducked down again and looked at Susie. 'She didn't see me,' he whispered.

Susie grunted, trying to overcome the shivers that were beginning to run up and down her spine, making her quiver all over. Martha was squatting passively on a kneeler, apparently content just to wait and be told what to do next, but suddenly she moved her arm.

A pile of prayer-books, balanced precariously on the ledge, tumbled to the floor.

William and Susie froze. There was a light tapping sound of high heels on a stone floor, moving down the church towards them: once it hesitated for a moment, and then came on. And then, without warning, the whole building rang with noise, an echoing clamour that lifted from floor to ceiling and flung itself from wall to wall: the clock was striking.

The children scuttled the length of the pew and darted across the central aisle, glimpsing as they fled a dark figure in the shadows that stopped and changed direction as it saw them. They slithered through another pew, and when the noise faded away and the silence returned to the church they were huddled together behind the bulk of a round pillar.

The jangle of the bells ebbed right away, and the church was still again. It seemed to enfold its own silence: from somewhere outside, far away as though in another world, came the voices of children and the putter of a car engine. The bluebottle zigzagged up and down a window, a pew creaked, and, nearer, something brushed against a chair and there was the whisper of a movement on the floor.

They stayed behind the pillar until they could stand it no longer: when they could feel Morgan's approach in the dreadful chill stealing into their bones, and hear the hiss of her breath, they fled away down the side aisle in the direction of the entrance. But Morgan moved parallel to them, down the centre. Out of the corner of her eye, across the expanse of empty pews, Susie caught sight of her moving purposefully, her heels clicking on the stone, her head turned towards the children, watching them.

They stopped behind another pillar. Yards away, a new sound reached them, through air and stone: Morgan was laughing. Then a voice, low and husky, said, 'Martha, come here.'

Martha said apologetically, 'I'm afraid I've got to go now.' She shook Susie's hand from her arm, stepped away from the pillar and began to walk down the aisle towards the door, and Morgan moved to meet her.

They were all at the top of the church now. Martha rounded the corner of the last pew and began to walk across the wide, bare space between the entrance and the rows of pews in the main body of the building.

Susie said, in a voice that sounded deep and hollow, bouncing off the stone, 'Stop, Martha! Stop! Don't go near her!' But Martha seemed not to hear.

Desperately, the others left the security of the pillar and began to run after her. William had a wild notion of grabbing Martha and pulling her back, but Morgan was still between them and the door. He wondered again if he could find the courage to attack her, and knew in the same instant that what had worked once would not do so again. Morgan was gaining in strength all the time.

Morgan had reached the end of the centre aisle, and had turned to meet Martha. Light from a window high above their heads fell coldly on her white face and the black discs of her glasses. She had no expression. Suddenly she hesitated for a moment, and drew in her breath sharply, taking a quick sideways step as she did so. Susie looked down, and saw that there was a brass memorial cross let into the stone floor just in front of her feet.

She used to be confounded by the sign of the Cross . . .

Susie looked round wildly. There was a huge silver one on an altar in the chapel behind her. Too big – she could never lift it. But on a pillar beside the door there was another, made of straw, probably left over from last year's Harvest Festival. The stem and arms were beautifully plaited in a diamond pattern, with a fringe of corn ears at the ends. Susie grabbed hold of it and ran forward, pushing it blindly in front of her, knocking Martha aside as she did so.

Morgan hissed like a snake, and recoiled. And then she screamed, and the sound filled the church like a swelling cloud, ringing against the pillars and soaring up to the roof until it trailed away into a thin shriek that ran like something live high above their heads under the vaulting and the slit windows at the top of the walls. And then it, too, was gone, and so was Morgan. The children were standing alone, staring at the spot where she had been.

Susie hung the straw cross back on its hook on the pillar, adjusting it carefully so that it hung straight. She took Martha by the hand and they all three moved out into the clattering, everyday world of the street.

As soon as they were clear of the church, Susie said, 'We've got to do something about Martha.' Martha, at the sound of her name, looked up in surprise, but said nothing.

'What can we do?'

'We'll take her to the hospital,' said Susie with energy. 'To the Casualty. Maybe they'll be able to do something about her, and anyway it's not a bad place to hide from Morgan.'

William nodded agreement: it seemed a sensible move. He remembered Miss Hepplewhite's words 'She cannot abide reason'. He wondered for a moment what Miss Hepplewhite was doing, in her big house and peaceful garden, and if she knew what was happening to them, and then he hurried after Susie.

They both knew the Casualty Department at the hospital: William from the time he fell off the church wall and broke his wrist, and Susie from the time her little brother was thought to have eaten half a bottle of aspirins, which were later found pushed behind a cushion on the settee. They turned through the big double doors of the hospital and Susie paused at the reception desk, with Martha in tow.

A nurse looked up from some papers and smiled pleasantly. 'Will you sit down over there, dear,' she said. 'Someone will be with you in a moment.'

They sat in a row on chairs against the wall. There were other people around, also waiting: a man with a grubby bandage tied round his head, others less visibly injured. From time to time a nurse, or a doctor in a white coat, appeared from behind swing doors, and spoke to someone, or led them away. There was no atmosphere of crisis: from behind a door somewhere cups rattled, and someone laughed.

After a few minutes a short, cheerful-looking nurse, billowing like a cushion above and below her wide black belt, came through the glass doors and approached them. 'What's the trouble, dear?' she asked, addressing all three of them.

'It's her,' said Susie, giving Martha a nudge. 'She's behaving all funny. Like she wasn't quite with us.'

The nurse smiled kindly at Martha and bent down a little. 'Are you feeling all right, dear?'

Martha stared at her, and said nothing.

The nurse turned to Susie. 'Has she had a bang on the head, dear?' she asked.

'Don't think so,' said Susie. Then added hastily, 'Least as far as I know she hasn't. She might have.'

'I see.' The nurse began to examine Martha, straightening her arms and legs and running her hands over her head. 'Where's your mother, dear? Why didn't she come with you?'

'She's shopping,' said Susie, quickly, seeing that William was about to say something. 'We've got to meet her in an hour. In the market square.'

The nurse looked slightly puzzled, but said nothing. She asked for their names and address: Susie unblushingly announced them to be John, Dawn and Sheila Porter, of Steeple Hampden.

'I can't find anything wrong with your sister, my dear,' said the nurse. 'But she does seem a bit dazed. I think we'd better have one of the doctors have a look at her. Let's take her along to one of the cubicles.'

She held out her hand to Martha, but Susie got up firmly and said, 'We'll all come.'

The nurse led them through the swing doors and into a long passage, with curtained cubicles at either side of it. Her shoes squeaked on the shiny linoleum and there was a smell of medicines and ether. A long way away someone was using an electric polisher and singing. The nurse ushered them into a cubicle, made Martha lie down on a couch, and told them to wait. They sat in silence, William feeling very uncomfortable, and acutely aware of his torn jeans and dirty Plimsolls. Susie sat bolt upright, her mouth in a tight, straight line.

After a minute or two the curtains parted and a man came in. He wore a white coat, with pencils and pens sticking out of a breast pocket, and a stethoscope round his neck. He was very dark-skinned, with a thin, bony face and brown, thick-lashed eyes. Indian or something, thought William. A metal label pinned to his coat said 'Dr Chatterjee'.

He smiled quickly at Susie and William and bent over Martha, saying reassuring things. He poked and prodded her, peered into her eyes with a light, listened to her chest, turned her head from side to side.

'Does that hurt?'

'No,' said Martha politely. 'I'm not hurting anywhere.' She lay on the couch, and stared up at him. She seemed to be taking a little more interest in things.

The nurse, hovering in the background, said, 'Her sister doesn't think she's had a fall. I thought perhaps some kind of delayed shock . . .'

The doctor ignored her. He said to Susie, 'How long has she been like this?'

Susie leaned forward. It was a little difficult to catch what he said; he spoke very fast, with the accents on words in unexpected places. 'All day, really. She got up like that this morning.'

The doctor tapped his teeth with the end of the pencil, thoughtfully, and shone his torch again into Martha's eyes. He had very beautiful hands, with long, delicate fingers, tilted upwards at the ends. 'If we were in my country,' he said, speaking very fast, 'I would say that she had come under the influence of some evil person. I have seen this kind of thing before.'

The nurse's shoes squeaked on the floor: her face was a mask of disapproval. But Susie said cautiously, 'I think I know what you mean.'

The doctor looked at her for a moment and then said, 'Would you like to tell me about it?'

'No, thank you,' said Susie, 'I don't think it would help.'

Martha, from the couch, suddenly announced that she was thirsty. The doctor patted her arm kindly and put the torch back in his pocket.

The nurse said in a very frosty voice, 'What am I to put for the diagnosis, then?'

Dr Chatterjee said, 'If that is worrying you very much, just put "Temporary hypnotic state". Fortunately it is already beginning to pass. Let her rest here for a while, and bring her a cup of tea. Then she can go home.'

'Thank you,' said Susie.

'Not at all. I am very pleased to have met you.' He shook hands with them, gravely, and went out.

The nurse was bursting with indignation. She bustled in and out, muttering that she had never heard such nonsense in all her life, and you never knew where you were with some of these foreign doctors. Martha sat up, sipping tea.

Suddenly she said, in a very ordinary voice. 'Where am I?'

'In Chipping Ledbury hospital,' said William.

'Gosh, why? Have I had an accident?' She began to feel herself, gingerly.

'No. But you've been behaving all funny. We think Morgan got you.'

'Morgan!' Martha's eyes widened and she swung her legs off the couch. 'When? How?'

'Don't you remember?' said Susie sharply. 'You went off in the car with her, to that house.'

Martha gaped. 'I don't remember anything. How did we get here? I want to go home.'

'So do we. But it's difficult. You see, Morgan's here somewhere, looking for us.'

Martha was staring at the floor, frowning. 'I don't remember anything about today,' she said, 'but there was something funny about last night. I remember I woke up and looked out of the window, and there was a huge wind, and – I saw the Stones.'

'The Stones?' said William blankly. 'How could you? You can't see them from your house.'

'That's just it. They were moving.'

The others stared at her, awed. 'Moving?' said William, in wonder.

'And there was something else,' said Martha, screwing up her face in an effort of concentration. 'But I can't remember what it was . . .'

'Never mind,' said Susie, getting up. 'Let's try and get to the bus station before she finds us again.'

They went out into the passage. At the same moment the nurse came through the swing doors. 'Ah!' she said brightly. 'I was just coming to have a look at you. Feeling all right now, dear?'

'Yes, thank you,' said Martha. 'Quite all right.'

'There's a good girl. Well, you're in luck. You're going to have a lift home. There's a kind lady here saying she'll take you all the way in her car.'

The children looked at each other. Susie stiffened. 'A lady?'

'That's it, dear.' The nurse was ushering them before her through the doors as she talked. 'Ever such a nice lady. And she got a lovely car – I saw it. Really grand. I'd say you were lucky children.'

They were through the doors now. At the far side of the room, by the entrance, past the reception desk and the rows of seated people waiting, there was someone standing, half-hidden from them by a screen.

'We aren't allowed to go with strangers,' said Susie tensely.

'Quite right, dear. But this'll be all right, I promise you that. You see, the lady isn't a stranger. We know who she is – she's a Mrs Steel, who lives just outside the town. Everybody knows her husband.'

'All the same, I think we'll take the bus,' said Susie. They were all three staring towards the entrance.

William said, boldly, 'Anyway, why does she want to give us a lift?'

The nurse was looking put out. 'Well, it's very kind of her, isn't it? I don't think you ought to talk like that. She said something about a message from your mother.'

'She doesn't know our mothers,' said Martha. 'We're not going with her.'

Susie opened her mouth to say 'Mother' but the nurse had not noticed Martha's mistake. 'Oh, dear,' she said in distress, 'you are being difficult. I don't know what to say. It's most awkward. I don't want to offend

Mrs Steel, with her husband being on the hospital management committee.' She looked at the children despairingly.

There was a rumbling sound. An ambulance man was pushing an empty stretcher on a trolley towards the exit. The figure in the doorway moved aside to let him pass, stepping back outside. As it did so the daylight fell on its pale skin and shining hair, and the hooded eyes turned towards them. William suddenly said, 'Run!', and they dashed after the man with the trolley and shot through the door in his wake, with the nurse making protesting noises and the waiting people turning to stare after them. They passed within a couple of yards of Morgan, and Susie thought that she put out a hand towards them, but then they were down the steps and running fast away down the street towards the bus station.

They ran the whole way, without looking behind them. It was raining quite hard, spearing the pavements and streaming from the gutters, and passers-by hurried with heads down, half-buried under their umbrellas. Nobody looked at them, and there was no sound of following footsteps.

The Steeple Hampden bus was standing in its bay, with the engine running. Gasping with relief, they climbed in and sat down on seats right at the back. A number of familiar faces looked up, and registered their arrival. In the seat in front were two neighbours, chatting comfortably under a welter of shopping-baskets and parcels. One of them turned round.

'What are you up to, all on your own, Susie? And Martha, too?'

'Shopping for Mum,' said Susie quickly. She turned to stare out of the steamy window, hoping to forestall further questions. The woman turned round again and resumed her conversation.

The bus was warm and damp inside. Water trickled down the misted windows, and outside the rain pattered on the shiny tarmac of the bus station. Susie rubbed a clear patch on the window and they all three stared out anxiously.

'Please may it go soon . . .' prayed Martha, under her breath.

At last the conductor appeared, strolling idly towards the bus. He stopped to chat to a friend, while the children watched, agonized. He climbed onto the platform, but still they waited. And then at last the driver appeared: doors slammed, there was a comforting roar of engines, and they were moving slowly out onto the open road away from the town.

The children kept turning to stare out of the window as they left the town. Cars following the bus would hang behind for a few moments and then sweep past, water from the wet road spraying up under their tyres. The bus rumbled on, a warm, self-contained world of its own, stopping now and then to let people get on and off: the children began to feel safe and Martha found herself wishing the journey would never end. But they were already entering the valley: familiar landmarks loomed up on either side, a wood, spilling down the hillside into the fields, a group of cottages, a farm. Martha rubbed her arm over the window to clean it again and peered out: the countryside, faintly distorted by glass and steam, seemed to ripple a little like something seen under water. And the sky swept down to meet it all around – a dark, disturbed sky, full of rain and rough, jagged clouds. She looked back along the shining road. A line of cars had formed behind the slow-moving bus, and the fourth one was larger than the others, and black.

She gave a startled cry, and the others turned round. They all three stared back, and as they did so the black car slid past the one in front of it, and moved one place nearer to the bus.

'Oh, gosh!' said Susie in dismay.

The car behind turned off down a side road. There was a further change of places, and now the Rolls was directly behind the bus. They were looking straight down into it.

'I say!' said William, in a shaken, disbelieving voice, 'there isn't anyone driving it.'

It was perfectly true. The Rolls slid silently behind the bus, at a level speed, and although the light was bad they could see quite well into it. No one sat behind the steering-wheel, but behind the glass partition, in the back seat, there was a glimpse of a pair of crossed legs, and hands folded in a lap.

'It can't . . .' said William, but the girls said nothing. Clearly it could.

'Now I get it about the chauffeur,' whispered Susie. Martha stared at her in perplexity, and then looked back at the car.

William leaned forward and tapped the shoulder of the woman in front of him. 'Excuse me,' he said politely, 'but do you see that car behind the bus?'

The woman lifted herself slightly in her seat and craned her head over her shoulder to look out of the window.

'Yes, my dear? Oh – yes, it is a grand-looking car, isn't it? Very big. Mad about cars, are you? Just like my grandson – it's always "Look at that, Gran" and "Look at this". Boys are all the same, aren't they?' She beamed kindly at him and turned back to her companion.

'No,' said William, 'it's not that. Can you see anything funny about it?'

The woman looked round again, a shade impatiently. 'No, dear, I can't say I can. But then I don't know anything about cars.'

The children looked at each other. Into Martha's head swam something she had heard Miss Hepplewhite say. 'People see only what they expect to see: we can no longer endure the unexplained.'

Nine

The bus crept through the valley, beneath swollen clouds and between hedges stooping under the rain. The fields rolled away on either side, the ripe barley parched-looking even now, with poppies sparkling in the hedgerows among foaming meadow-sweet and the stiff dried heads of cow-parsley. Ahead, where the road looped inwards a little, away from the river and towards the sloping hills, Steeple Hampden waited, the church spire pointing upwards to the sky from among the crouching houses. And beyond the village, still and watching in their fold of the hill, with the elms stark against the sky behind them and the soft grass lapping their feet, the Stones must be standing, where they had always stood and perhaps always would stand.

Or so Martha thought, swaying from side to side with the movement of the bus and fearfully watching the black car as it kept its even pace behind. The Stones were much in her thoughts, though she could not explain why, even to herself. It was all to do with last night, and with something else that kept escaping her – something that she felt certain had happened but which had become all misty and elusive, like a name or a face remembered and yet forgotten. She scowled and bit her lip, trying to drag whatever it was back into her mind.

They passed the barn, and Miss Hepplewhite's house. Susie said, 'We ought to go and tell her Martha's all right. She was ever so worried.'

'Was she?' said Martha, flattered.

'We all were, silly. But you don't need to get cocky about it now. It was us rescued you, wasn't it?'

'Thank you very much,' said Martha.

'It's all right.'

William was staring out of the back window. 'She's still there,' he said. 'I don't see how we can go to Miss Hepplewhite's. We'd have to go back past her, wouldn't we?'

'What's she at?' said Susie uneasily.

'I know jolly well what she's at. She's hunting us now, that's what. Before it was the other way, us attacking her, and rescuing Martha. Now she's turned it all round.'

There was a silence, broken only by the throb of the bus and little gusts of chatter from the other passengers. Martha said in a tight voice, 'I wish Miss Hepplewhite was here, I do really.'

'I don't think she can help any more. I reckon we've got to do this by ourselves.'

The bus pulled up outside the pub, and the black car stopped behind it. The children got off reluctantly, keeping close to other people. The village street was deserted: rain pricked the tarmac and dripped from cottage gutters. The other passengers hurried away without glancing at either the car or the children. The bus engine roared as it prepared to move off again.

'Come on,' said Susie, 'we got to go straight on – there's nothing else we can do.' She cast a longing look backwards at the security of the shop, beyond the evil bulk of the Rolls. Bet Mum could deal with her, she thought. Or could she . . .

They began to walk down the road, glancing unhappily over their shoulders from time to time. The Rolls followed, moving slowly but narrowing the gap between them all the time. It was enormous, almost filling the street.

'What's she at?' said Susie again, and Martha began to whimper. They were half-running now, and the car was coming on steadily behind them.

They were level with the last group of cottages in the village: beyond that were the open fields of the valley, with the Sharnbrook away to one side and the slope of the hill on the other.

'We've got to stop,' said William in a frantic voice. 'Get help. Not out there . . .'

They scrambled towards the last cottage, and Susie hammered on the door. The Rolls slowed down, and stopped. The door opened and old Mrs Tomkins, the postman's wife, looked out.

Susie said hysterically, 'Please can we come in? That car – it's going to run us over – it's following us. Please let us in.'

'Now, now,' said Mrs Tomkins. 'What car?' She unlatched the door with maddening slowness, and stared down the road.

'That one. The black one.'

'But it's stopped. Just standing there, it is. What's wrong with that?'

'It'll start again,' said William, 'if we go on. Honestly. *Please* can we come in?'

'Now who'd want to do a thing like that? Run you over, indeed!'

'She would. Oh, please . . .'

'Now that's a silly thing to say, Susie. If this is a joke I don't think it's at all funny. I've a good mind to tell your mother. Now run along home, all of you.'

The door closed. There was a cough and a murmur as the engine of the Rolls started up again.

'I said we were on our own,' said William. 'Us and her.' He looked at Susie, very white.

'We got to get off the road,' said Susie. 'That's what. Into the fields. Then if she comes after us at least it won't be the car as well.'

There was a gate at the side of the road, opening into a field. Ripe barley rolled away down to the river, stroked by the wind. They swarmed over the gate and into the field with the stiff heads of barley rattling all around them: bent under its own weight and much flattened by summer storms, it did not offer much cover. They crept along, not far from the hedge, and through breaks in the thorn and bramble they could see the dark shape of the Rolls moving silently along the road, shadowing them.

'We've been daft,' said Susie, 'coming in here. Now we're trapped, like.'

'Look,' said William, 'why don't we make a dash for it down to the river. Then we could hide in the bushes along the edge and make a circle back to the village.'

'She'd see.'

'Yes. But we've got a start. She couldn't catch up. By the time she'd got out of the car we'd be half-way there.'

Susie hesitated. 'All right. We got to do something. You all right, Martha?'

'Yes,' said Martha faintly, 'I'm all right.'

'Come on, then.' They turned and began to run across the field, the barley tugging against them. After a minute or so they paused, and looked back.

'Oh, no!' cried William in horror.

The Rolls had reached a point where there was another gate into the field from the road. It was closed. The car stopped, and then it began to turn. It seemed to gather itself, and then, with a great, noiseless burst of power it speeded up and smashed straight into the gate. It went through it like a tank, scattering splintered timber into the air, and ploughed right on, cutting a great swath through the barley.

The children tore on across the field. The car was several hundred yards behind them, but it was getting closer all the time. The wet corn lashed against them, soaking their clothes and dragging against their legs, making it difficult to run fast. They found themselves moving slowly and heavily, like swimmers, and all the time the car was forging after them, crushing the corn under its great weight and spraying flocks of startled birds up into the air all around it. They ran now without looking behind them, trying to pick the easiest way across the field and avoid tripping on the hard ruts: ahead of them a line of willows marked the course of the Sharnbrook, very near to the bridge where they had fished earlier. Behind them the rumble and thump of the car, banging over the hard ground, came nearer all the time. Martha, glancing up for a moment, saw a thunderous sky pressing down on the valley and ahead a great swinging curtain of rain blotted out the fields on the other side of the river.

'The river bank ...' panted William. 'Get to the river bank ...'

The car was close behind them now. They could feel rather than hear the throb of its engine, and the ground seemed to shake under its great weight. The river was twenty yards away – fifteen – ten – and now they were in the tangled growth on the lip of the bank. William glanced back and saw the outline of a figure in the back of the car, leaning forward.

'I can't go in the water!' cried Martha, frantically. 'It's too deep ... I can't swim ...'

She hesitated, panic-stricken, but William shouted over his shoulder, 'Come on! It'll be all right. I know this bit – there's a ledge. Jump, Martha, jump!'

She jumped, shutting her eyes, and feeling wet branches grabbing at her legs and Susie panting beside her. They slithered down the bank after William, with the river, quite wide at this point and running fast and brown between the banks, only a yard below them. Martha clutched at Susie in terror as she fell, expecting to be swept away in the cold water and, instead, felt firm ground under her feet, with the river still a foot or two away.

They had jumped onto a shallow ledge, invisible from the field and overhung by the bank above.

'Get back!' said William, and they all crouched back against the sticky clay of the bank.

There was a fearful noise above them, and chunks of

the bank began to fall away, tumbling all about them. And, over their very heads, the black bulk of the car came lurching and tipping down into the river. It moved sluggishly, like something in a slow-motion film, carried forward by its own weight, and the shining bonnet was already touching the water as the back wheels left the bank. There was a tremendous splash: water and mud surged up to their knees and the ground rocked. Slowly the great car sank down into the river, with the water boiling and sucking all around it and waves slapping up against the banks on either side.

And, as the thing happened, the rain-storm sweeping across the valley reached the Sharnbrook, darkening everything, so that the last moments of the car were obscured by the driving, lashing rain, and a crack of thunder running right across the sky above the valley drowned every other noise. Lightning sizzled on the roof of the car as it sank further into the water.

Or was it lightning? The children, huddled together in terror, staring out across the river, saw it, and afterwards were never certain. There was light, that was sure, and something crackled, and the air was filled with shrill hissing, and they all felt a tingling on their arms and in the scalp. And then the car was gone, and the rain was beating down onto the water and pouring from the crumbling bank down their backs, and overhead the thunder was rolling backwards and forwards across the sky.

And something else. Another noise that was not thunder. Susie heard it first, and leaned forward, peering upwards, the rain coursing down her face. It seemed to come from the air somewhere above the river, just above where the car had sunk. A wailing, thin and high, beginning as a moan and then rising to a shriek, dying away into the steady patter of the rain. A manic, hideous sound: a sound that sent a shudder down her spine.

Martha heard it, and stiffened, and then suddenly cried, 'Don't listen! Put your hands over your ears! I remember now – that's the noise I heard in the night – and then everything went like in a dream. We mustn't listen!' She clapped her hands over her ears and leaned forward, burying her head in her lap. The others stared, silenced by the urgency in her voice, and then they did the same, as the scream rose again over the river.

They crouched there for minutes, fingers jammed in their ears so that they could hear nothing but the thump of their own hearts, and then, cautiously, William took his hands away and sat up. The noise had gone. The thunder still roamed the sky, but further away now, and the rain was falling less heavily. The top of the car was just visible under the surface of the river, like a shining submerged rock. He nudged the girls.

'It's all right. It's gone.'

Martha gave a great sigh. Her hair was plastered down on her head, making her face look even thinner and bonier than usual, and her eyes enormous. 'Oh, that horrible noise! That's what I heard before – and I *listened* to it for ages.' She shuddered.

Susie, wringing the water from her plait, said, 'D'you think she's gone?'

None of them even suggested that Morgan might have vanished with the car: they knew too well that she had not.

'Not far,' said William. 'I can still feel her.' He looked round uneasily.

All of a sudden Martha said, with a kind of excitement, 'I'm beginning to remember all sorts of things – about last night, and this morning.'

'Such as?' asked Susie.

'Well, this morning, when she talked to me by the bridge, I said something about the Stones – I can't quite remember why now – and she was all funny about them. As though – as though she was afraid of them.'

'Afraid of them?' said William, staring.

'Yes. She said something about it being a bad place up there, and we mustn't go there.'

'It isn't,' said Susie, 'it's good up there. I like it better than anywhere in the valley.'

'So do I. But she doesn't. And last night – when I looked out of the window – and saw them, I had the feeling that it was all something to do with her. They looked like an army getting ready for a battle, somehow. I know it sounds a bit silly,' she added apologetically.

'I don't think it does,' said William. 'It's made me think of something Mr Sampson said once, only I wasn't really listening when he said it. Something about them being Knights, and a battle with a bad queen. It sounded like a load of rubbish, but now I think he must've been talking about Morgan.'

They all sat, thoughtful, quite unconscious of their soaked clothes and chilled limbs. They thought of the Hampden Stones, and the peaceful stillness up there, with the valley stretched out below, and they thought of Morgan, with her snake head and her eyes that were not human, and the sense of terror that she carried with her, and to all of them came the idea, quite simply:

137

they are against each other, they are the opposite sides of things.

'Should we go there?' said Susie. She was thinking, as were the others, that there, of all places, they would be safe.

William nodded. They got up and scrambled up the bank. When they reached the top they were all three streaked all over with mud and clay. The rain had almost stopped but thunder still rolled distantly and the clouds hung low. They made their way up the barley field again, keeping close to the hedge: right across the field lay the path cut by the car. William thought for a moment that people were going to wonder about that when they saw it, and then forgot about it: people, and the village, and what it did and thought, didn't seem to matter any more. They were no longer in the same world.

They kept looking round nervously, but there was no sign of Morgan. The wind had dropped, and the fields were very still, and the birds were silent, in the way that birds are silent in the minutes before a thunderstorm. The children could hear only the tramp of their own feet: there was not even a car on the road, or an aeroplane in the sky. The combine harvester that had been working its way round a field on the other side of the river seemed to have gone. They walked on, one behind the other. Once William said, 'I didn't realize it was so far to the road.'

'Oh, do go on,' said Susie. 'Let's get up to the Stones quickly.'

After another five minutes William said, 'We haven't gone the wrong way, have we?'

They had passed out of the barley field into a curious area of scrubland that none of them could remember seeing before. The grass was long and coarse, dotted with thorn bushes: it was unlike any field in the valley that they had ever seen. And there were far too many trees around. Patches of woodland stretched in all directions, and when they looked back they could no longer see the river. William felt dizzy for a moment.

'I can't think how we've missed the road,' he said.

Bewildered, they hurried on. There was dense woodland on their right, but they avoided that and kept to the patchy bits of more open country. Ahead of them, the line of the hill at the side of the valley was as it should be, but there were too many trees sprawling down the sides of it, and the dark lines of the hedges had gone. Looking to the left, in the direction of the village, they could not find the familiar landmark of the church spire.

'Something's gone awfully wrong,' said Martha, in a frightened voice.

Beyond them, a brown animal, like some kind of deer, skittered from behind a clump of thorn bushes and vanished among the trees.

Thunder crashed nearer, and it began to rain. And, above the thunder, that curdling scream came whistling down the valley again and, instinctively, they clapped their hands over their ears and began to run.

They were leaving the floor of the valley now and climbing the slope of the hill in the direction of the place where the Stones ought to be. Suddenly Susie took her hands away from her ears and pointed.

'Look! There's a sort of road.'

It was a track of beaten earth, quite wide, slanting straight as a die up the hillside, cutting through trees and bushes. And it led precisely where they wanted to go.

Martha cried in astonishment, 'It's our road! The old road to the Stones!' The scream came once again, whipping over their heads, and then ceasing abruptly.

They were running up the road now, and it was easier going on the packed earth. Lightning shone somewhere behind the hill, and was gone again. Martha felt a deadly chill now and there was a drumming in her ears that seemed to get louder all the time. She swallowed, and took a deep breath, but still it pounded, and suddenly she knew it was not inside her at all but somewhere behind. She looked round at the same moment as the others, and they all saw the same thing.

Far behind, in the bed of the valley, where the pale scar of the road bent a little and then led away towards the south, where the rooftops of Chipping Ledbury should be, but were not, there was something moving fast, and gathering speed all the time. It was a white horse, and it carried a dark rider, and the dreadful beat of its hooves already made the ground tremble under their feet. Near to it, they could see now the glint of the Sharnbrook, tracing its familiar loops and curves between the willows and alders, and where the village should have been there was a confusion of round shapes in a grassy space, and smoke curling up from open fires.

But they could not stop to look: the drumming hoof-beats came nearer, and the rider bent forward over the flying mane to urge the creature on. They turned, and fled up the hillside.

They were stumbling with tiredness, and the ground seemed to lurch and sway in front of their very eyes. Their breath came in short, painful gasps. For Martha, it held all the terror of a dream pursuit, with her limbs growing heavier and heavier as the beating of those hooves approached and the noise of the horse's snorting crept up the hill. And with it, another sound. A voice, calling her. A deep, woman's voice shouting, 'Martha! Martha!'

'No!' Martha shouted back. 'No! No! No! I'm not coming with you any more!' But her breathless voice came only as a whisper, addressed to the ground, and Susie, running beside her, did not even look up.

The brow of the hill was within reach now, and beyond it, if there was anything familiar left in this distorted landscape, should lie the piece of level ground where the Stones stood. The line of elms to the right was no longer there: instead was the smoky outline of a dense wood, crouched against the skyline like a sleeping animal. The children, feeling the slope of the hill under their feet grow more gradual, looked ahead of them with a great hope, and for a moment forgot the pounding of the hooves behind them.

Above the hill, thunderclouds were piled in the sky like castles and cathedrals, grey against grey, shifting and tearing all the time, sometimes wildly lit by the silent lightning. And below, very still, in calm repose against the sharp green of the grass, stood the Stones. They seemed to have grown a little, and their outlines were sharper and bore suggestions of the axe, and there was something wrong about their arrangement. The two on the far side that should be toppled at an angle were not, and the one that formerly lay half under the hedge, apart from its fellows, now stood in its place in the circle. The central slab, lying sunk in the grass, was where it should be, but there was something standing in front of it.

The children slowed up. Martha gave a startled gasp and clutched at Susie's arm. The sky had grown so dark that, from the hundred yards or so that still separated them from the Stones, it was impossible to see at all clearly. Was it human? Alive?

It took a step forward, and they saw that it was a woman. She stretched out her arm and beckoned to them.

'She wants us to come,' said William uncertainly.

Susie said, in a scared voice, 'It might be a trick.'

'Morgan's behind us. How can she be in front as well?'

Above them the sky roared. Rain came sheeting down, drifting in great veils across the Stones, and above the noise the scream came again, swooping low over their heads, and the snorting of the horse was very near now, flying up the road behind them. Martha began to moan.

Lightning flared, and hung for a moment over the whole hilltop. And in that moment they saw the face of the woman ahead of them.

Susie said, in pure astonishment, 'Miss Hepple-white!' But it was a question as much as an assertion: she was not sure. The face was young, and although it offered sanctuary, it carried with it also a total strangeness, a suggestion of something very old and far away: and yet, despite all this, there was something there that they had seen before. And then the light went, and with it the figure. The Stones were there, but the circle was empty. And the hoofbeats pounded the hillside.

'Come on!' cried William.

They ran, and as they covered the last stretch to the Stones, the thunder of the hooves met the clamour of the sky above. The whistle of mane and tail flying through the air joined the hissing of Morgan's breath as she leaned forward on the horse's neck, and as they flung themselves between the two nearest of the Stones, they felt the whole circle move, and where the place had been through which they fled there was no space, but only a grey wall of stone beyond which the horse raged and Morgan's scream rang down into the valley and back again.

They lay face down in the grass, not daring to move or look up, and around and above them the battle roared. There was the terrible crash of stone against stone, the whistle of steel in the air, the screech of steel on stone, and the piercing shrieks of Morgan's fury and frustration. And above it all the thunder played out its own battle. Once Martha dared to roll over a little and look up, and it seemed to her that the whole sky was in a ferment, and that the flowing shapes of the clouds were the shapes of some strange and monstrous chase that raged back and forth above the valley, and then she glimpsed another flying shape, and felt the awesome movement of the Stones, and knew that they were in the middle of something it was not good to watch. She hid her face again, and waited.

The battle swept to and fro above them, rocking the very ground they lay on. They had the feeling that heavy bodies passed within inches of them, avoiding crushing them only by a miracle, and sometimes the crashes and shrieks were only a yard or two above their heads. And then, amid a crescendo of noise, there was a terrible, mounting wail of rage and despair.

William, eyes closed on blackness, his ears ringing with noise, thought: the Stones have won at last.

The wail rose up into the air, and swept away down

the valley, trailing off into the distance. For long minutes they could still hear it, fading and fading, and then it was gone altogether. The trembling ground subsided, the Stones were still, and the children lay in peace.

It might have been a kind of sleep: they had the impression afterwards that they had lain there for a long time, longer even than the time of the battle itself. They all became aware of things again at about the same moment, and rolled over one by one, and sat up.

There was a rim of pale sky along the far side of the valley, and through breaks in the cloud shafts of light poured down onto the familiar green and yellow of the fields, and the dark lines of the hedges. The grey road, with cars crawling slowly like insects, followed the twists of the Sharnbrook, and a gleam of pale sunlight gilded the spire of the church.

Susie said, in her most matter-of-fact voice, 'Looks like it's clearing up.'

William realized that he was extremely hungry: he looked at his watch, but it had stopped at half past nine. Was it morning or afternoon? Impossible to tell: the sun was still hidden behind clouds.

Martha stood up, and walked cautiously round the Stones. They were all in their usual places, slippery with rain. The tall one at the back was still scarred where some ill-mannered person had carved a name and a date on it. The fallen ones lay once again on their sides. She turned, and saw that Susie and William were also staring in bewilderment. William's lips moved, counting. Then he shook himself briskly, like a dog, and said, 'I think we'd better go and find Miss Hepplewhite.'

The three children set off down the hill, rain-soaked and streaked with mud from the river. They took the track by the hedge. The old road was again blotted out beneath the barley, not even the ghost of it visible any more.

Ten

By the time they reached Miss Hepplewhite's garden
the sun had come out. All the way there the valley had
been coming to life after the storm, the birds no longer
clinging like old rags to the trees and bushes but busy
again in the corn, the rooks sweeping the sky, the sod-
den grass beginning to lift itself. In Miss Hepplewhite's garden the battered roses hung down, and
water coursed off the roof from the gutters. Her cat
paced the terrace, lifting fastidious feet.

Miss Hepplewhite opened the door to their
knock, and from behind her came the heavy smell of
jam.

'I can see you have been a long way,' she said at last,
after studying them for almost a minute. 'And I cannot
recall ever being so pleased to see anyone. You had
better come in: we cannot return you to your parents
in this condition.'

They trailed muddily along the stone corridor to the
kitchen. Pots of jam, neatly labelled, were ranged in
rows all over the table, and the window-sill was littered
with sated wasps.

'I have been occupying myself,' said Miss Hepplewhite. 'But I must admit my thoughts were never on
what I was doing.' She swept the pots to one side, and
began to stack the table with plates of cakes and bis-
cuits, and fresh-cut bread and butter.

Susie, sitting down on a chair and looking round at it
all, said curiously, 'Were you expecting us?'

'Let us just say that I was hoping to see you, and at a

certain point my hopes became rather more substantial.'

Enough for her to start cutting the bread and butter, thought Susie. She stared at Miss Hepplewhite, almost accusingly, but Miss Hepplewhite had turned away and was saying with concern, 'I do hope you found shelter during that tiresome thunderstorm.'

'Miss Hepplewhite,' said Martha solemnly, 'have you been up on the hill today? At the Hampden Stones.'

Miss Hepplewhite's expression did not change, and she went on smiling, but there was a flicker of reserve in her eyes. 'The Stones? Ah, yes, a very pleasant spot. But I've not been there for a long time: the hill is too much for me nowadays.'

'How long?' asked Martha.

'Not for a very, very long time,' said Miss Hepplewhite firmly. 'Longer than I care to recall.' She began to draw chairs up to the table: clearly, the subject was closed.

As they ate, the children were able to sort things out. It was early afternoon, apparently. They all quailed a little at the thought of the explanations that were going to be expected from them when they got home, but for the moment there were more important things to be done.

Miss Hepplewhite listened avidly to the whole story. When they had finished she sat back with a sigh.

'You have done magnificently,' she said. 'The task is complete.'

'We didn't really do it alone,' said William. 'The Stones finished her off.'

'But you gave them the opportunity.'

We let her in, thought Martha, with that business in the barn, but perhaps in the end it was a good thing.

Maybe the Stones had been waiting for her. Or Miss Hepplewhite had. She stared at Miss Hepplewhite's face, the skin a fine tracery of wrinkles, like an old map, the features in calm repose, and searched for some reminder of the strange figure that had come and gone so quickly in the stone circle, and could find none. She sighed, and decided suddenly to pursue the matter no further. There were always some things you were never going to be sure about.

Susie also felt questions coming, and snapped an answer back at herself – 'Ask no questions and you'll be told no lies.' Instead, she said, 'What'll happen now about the road through the village?'

'I think,' said Miss Hepplewhite, 'we can assume that the affair will die a natural death now. It will be quite interesting to see how things resolve themselves, but I am not at all concerned as to the outcome.'

'Nobody'll ever know that it was us did it,' said William, a little sadly.

'Never mind. You will always have cause for self-congratulation. Private triumph is often the most satisfactory. And I shall know.'

'Will she ever come back?' asked Martha.

'Not in your time, my dears. She is never routed for ever, for of course she exists at different levels of time to you – to us. I don't think we need fear her any more at present. And her powers are growing less. That is why she clings to the things she is familiar with.'

A shadow on the wall, a touch of ice, a shriek in the wind, thundering hooves. Martha remembered, and looked gratefully round Miss Hepplewhite's warm, cluttered kitchen.

'All the same,' said William, 'she didn't do badly this time. That car . . .'

Susie, tucking into bread and butter, looked up suddenly and said, 'When was she last here?'

'Oh, dear me, let me see ... A couple of hundred years ago, it must have been, if I remember rightly. There were some other children – what were their names, now?'

The children leaned forward, intently. Susie put down the bread and butter on her plate, her mouth still open.

'It was through children that she found the way in then also. Of course it is always the larger things she is after, but children are so often more vulnerable to her.' Miss Hepplewhite sipped her tea thoughtfully. 'They drove her out, too, on that occasion.'

'Go on,' said William, 'what did they do?'

'My dear boy, it's a long story. Far too long to go into now – some other time, perhaps. And of course she was rampant in the seventeenth century – I must tell you about that some time ... But now I really think you must go home and reassure your no doubt half-demented parents. We are being most inconsiderate, sitting here chatting like this.'

They finished their meal, cleaned themselves up as best they could, though there was little they could do about their torn and mud-stained clothes, and said goodbye to Miss Hepplewhite. She stood at her front door, a small, stooping figure, in her long, old-fashioned dress and elaborate hat that no longer seemed ridiculous, and they turned to wave several times as they made their way down the drive.

'Just think,' said William, 'we'll be able to go up to the barn tomorrow, just like before all this began. Get on with things like that sledge.'

'You'd best remember that hammer then.'

149

'It wasn't me forgot it.'

'It jolly well was. Oh, never mind …' said Susie. Funny, she thought, we've not been getting at each other all day, William and me. Not like usually. We've been too busy, I s'pose.

Martha said, 'I'm going to get properly told off when my mum sees me. I've got a great tear all down my frock.'

'Me too. I'm not bothered, though. We been through worse today than being told off, haven't we?'

'You can say that again,' said William warmly. 'Pity we'll never be able to tell anyone about it. Not unless we want to get laughed at.'

They took the short cut through the churchyard. The long grass, soaked by the rain, brushed heavily against their legs and the tombstones were streaked with damp. The carved cherubs still joined hands above the name of Ebenezer Timms, died 1838, the rain-drops shining like tears on their bulbous cheeks, and the yawning gargoyle above the door spat water onto the stone step. The spire, bright apricot in the sunlight, shot straight up into the blue sky and far, far up at the top of it sparrows slipped in and out of the tiny slit windows near its point. Tits swung on the ropes of ivy that trailed from the top of the wall, and the big lime tree in the corner hummed softly, full of bees.

The children went through the gate and down the steps into the road. The wet tarmac was steaming a little in the sunshine and swallows looped over the stone rooftops. Everything was very quiet, but in the distance, outside Mrs Poulter's shop, there was activity. People were standing in groups, staring down the road towards the river, and pointing.

'Come on,' said Susie. 'There's something up.'

Mrs Poulter was standing amid a circle of neighbours, still in her shop overalls, looking down the road and talking excitedly. When she saw the children she burst into indignation.

'You are a naughty girl, Susie. I've been worried sick, let me tell you. And you, Martha Timms. Your mother's been to and fro all morning, half out of her mind. Where have you been, the lot of you? Do you know what time it is? Not back for your dinner, and not a word to anyone . . . It's too bad of you. And out in that shocking storm and all.'

'Sorry, Mum,' said Susie, with less defiance than usual. 'Sorry, I really am. What's everybody looking at?'

Mrs Poulter turned away for a moment, her irritation diverted. Further down the road the children could see two police cars parked, blue lights flashing, and a break-down lorry with a crane.

'There's been a horrible accident,' said Mrs Poulter, trying to conceal her relish. 'A car went into the river – down by the old bridge. It was that big Rolls – what belongs to Mr Steel at the Banton works. Seems someone drove it right across the field and slap into the river.'

'Goodness!' said William, in an unnatural voice. 'Whatever did they do that for?'

'That's what nobody knows. Seems it must have been stolen. They reckon there must've been someone in it. They're dragging the river – for bodies.'

'They won't find any,' said Susie calmly.

William said in a whisper, 'Shut up, Susie.'

'What's that?' said Mrs Poulter sharply. 'What do you know about it, miss?'

'Oh, nothing, really,' said Susie, but she had already drawn her mother's attention back to her, and the dreadful state of her hair and clothes. Clucking with anger, Mrs Poulter swept her daughter away into the shop, leaving William and Martha to make their way home and face their own problems of explanation.

The following morning the car had been lifted from the river and dragged back up the field, leaving a wide band of crushed barley in its wake. It was almost completely wrecked. It stood by the side of the road long enough for the people of Steeple Hampden to inspect it with ill-concealed satisfaction, and then it was towed away to Chipping Ledbury behind a lorry. The men who had been dragging the river piled their equipment into a van and went away, having found nothing.

'Didn't I say so?' said Susie, but not loud enough for her mother to hear. There had been enough trouble already.

William's father went into Chipping Ledbury by the afternoon bus, to see the editor of the *Gazette* about the road campaign. He came back an hour and a half later, clutching the early edition of the paper, almost speechless with excitement.

'What's up, Dad?' said William, but he had already guessed.

'Would you believe it! That blessed motorway's going the other way after all! And all because the factory's going to be closed down.' He flung the folded newspaper down on the kitchen table.

William picked it up. 'Must be because of your campaign really, Dad,' he said. 'I mean that Mr Steel must've had another think, mustn't he?'

'It says here he's retiring, or something. Still, I wonder ... It would be nice to think we had something to do with it.'

'Bet you did, Dad,' said William magnanimously. 'You and the whole village.'

A happy smile had crept across his father's face: they beamed at each other, and William began to read the newspaper. There was a small headline to one side of the front page which said 'Car Theft'. Underneath, he read: 'A Rolls Royce car belonging to Mr Steel of Clipsham Manor was found abandoned near Steeple Hampden last night, having been driven into the river Sharnbrook. The police assume that the car had been stolen, but are mystified as to how, or why, it got into the river, which lies a quarter of a mile from the road, across fields. At first it was feared that the driver of the car had been drowned, but frogmen dragging the river yesterday afternoon and this morning could find no trace of a body.'

On an inside page there was a large headline right across the top, and a picture of the village, taken from the main street looking towards the church. 'Sharnbrook Valley Reprieved?' William read. 'Those who have been concerned about the fate of the Sharnbrook valley, and the village of Steeple Hampden, will be relieved to hear that in all probability the M10 motorway will no longer be routed through the valley. This assumption can be made as a result of last night's unexpected news that the Steel and Potter factory at Banton is to be closed down, owing to the sudden retirement of the owner, Mr Steel.

'Mr Steel was not available to comment last night but Sir James Steel MP said that his brother's decision appeared to have been taken in some haste after his wife left suddenly from London Airport for the West Indies yesterday afternoon. It seems that Mrs Steel announced her intention to leave the UK to make her home permanently in Jamaica and her husband, who is 63, decided this morning to follow her. Since the closing-down of the factory disposes of any arguments against routing the motorway that side of Chipping Ledbury, it is reasonably safe to assume that the Sharnbrook valley is now reprieved and a treasured piece of England's heritage will, after all, be preserved for posterity.'

William tucked the newspaper under his arm and went out into the village to find the others. It was a fine, clear August morning. The countryside glistened, scoured by rain. All over the floor of the valley combine harvesters crawled back and forth, methodically circling the fields: above, the sky arched high and wide, a trail of vapour from an aeroplane vanishing into drifts of misty, fine-weather clouds. Outside the shop, the bread van stood, the engine running, the open doors revealing wire trays of bread and buns, and from the window of the room above the shop came the familiar sound of Susie arguing with her mother. William hesitated for a moment, and then moved on. Further down the road he could see the small figure of Martha, walking very slowly along beside the churchyard wall, her head cocked at a curious angle. He knew quite well what she was doing. She was looking upwards through the green canopy of the chestnut trees so that the sunlight, snapping down through the leaves, would half-dazzle her and give her a pleasurable, not-quite-there sensation. Then, like as not, she'd go and lie in the long grass of the churchyard and stare at the grey tombstones and the solid height of the spire. He shouted and waved, and Martha gave a little jump and hurried to meet him. There was another shout from behind, and Susie came out of the shop.

There were bright pink spots of indignation on her cheeks. 'You'd think my mum done it all herself, the way she goes on. Making out it was all that petition. And she was going on about how it wouldn't do any good, anyway.'

'It doesn't really matter,' said Martha. 'Does it? Not really.'

'All the same, I could tell her a thing or two.'

'You mustn't,' said William.

'I know,' said Susie, subsiding. It wasn't so bad, really, knowing something no one else knew, not even Mum. It made you feel good, somehow.

'Barn?' said William.

'Not straight away,' said Martha. 'First let's go ...'

'I know. To the Stones.'

'That's it,' said Susie. 'That's what I was thinking too. Just to see they're all right. It would be—' she searched for the right word '—respectful. Yes, that's it, respectful.'

The others nodded. They began to climb the hill. Cloud shadows rolled across the barley in front of them, and between the shadows, a still, faint trace, ran the line of a vanished road.

If you have enjoyed this PICCOLO Book you may like to choose your next book from the titles listed on the following pages.

Piccolo Fiction

also by Penelope Lively

ASTERCOTE   25p

Astercote village is dead . . . its ruins lie
hidden in the murky wood . . . But when
Peter and Mair Jenkins discover it, and its
secret Thing, Astercote starts to come mysteriously alive . . .

edited by Amabel Williams-Ellis
and Michael Pearson

TALES FROM THE GALAXIES   25p

Your imagination will boggle, your mind will
reel at these thrilling adventures of the planets,
spaceships, machines and weird creatures of
the future . . . a future that isn't perhaps so
very far away!

Julian R. Gregory and Roger Price

THE TOMORROW PEOPLE
in The Visitor   25p

From their secret HQ far beneath the streets
of London, Stephen, Kenny, Carol and John
– The Tomorrow People – set out on their
most exciting adventure – to discover the
identity and purpose of the mysterious visitor
from Outer Space. And danger isn't very far
behind . . .
(Based on the popular new TV series)

More Piccolo Fiction

Jonathan Gathorne-Hardy
**JANE'S ADVENTURES IN AND
OUT OF THE BOOK** (illus)   25p

When the resourceful Jane is left alone in her
parents' enormous castle, she goes exploring
. . . and in an old secret library she finds the
great Magic Book – which sets her off on the
most amazing adventures!

**JANE'S ADVENTURES ON THE
ISLAND OF PEEG** (illus)   25p

Peeg isn't an island until a shattering ex-
plosion severs it from the mainland and it
floats away – with Jane and her friends still
on it! The most extraordinary things happen
when the ingenious Jane has to cope with two
old soldiers who think the War is still on,
and the sinister Mr Tulip who plans to con-
quer the world.

Monica Dickens
**THE HOUSE AT WORLD'S
END** (illus)   25p

Rather than stay with niggling relatives in a
grey London suburb, the Fielding children –
Tom, Carrie, Em and Michael – decide to live
by themselves in a tumbledown country pub.
There are thrilling moments, and frightening
ones too, when the house at World's End becomes a haven for sick, stray or unwanted
animals.

SUMMER AT WORLD'S END
(illus)   25p

Now the Fielding children have settled into
World's End, still caring for any animal in
distress. This time, lack of money is a problem,
while some unwanted visitors add to the fun
– and the excitement.

Piccolo Non-Fiction

Now pit your wits and pick your brains and learn a whole lot besides with these ever-popular Piccolos!

Piccolo/TV Times
HOW A General Knowledge Question
and Answer Book (illus)   20p
If you want to know just HOW things are made, HOW things work, HOW things came about, then this is the book for you! It's based on the highly popular Southern TV series, and it's got all the answers to lots of interesting questions, from the way Vikings built their ships to the origin of April Fool's Day.

John Jaworski and Ian Stewart
NUT-CRACKERS (illus)   20p
Puzzles and games to boggle the mind! You'll find all sorts of things to do, things to make, and things to look at in this entertaining book – word games, string puzzles, mazes, codes, number patterns, skeleton crosswords – and not forgetting Professor Crankshaft's Impossible Objects!